SUGAR HERO

SUGAR DADDIES #15

CHARITY PARKERSON

--Warning: This book is intended for readers over the age of 18.

INTRODUCTION

HE IS ADRIK'S HERO. THEIR LOVE IS INEVITABLE.

Two and a half years ago, Detective Leo Humphrey swept in and saved Adrik from a monster. He gave Adrik his first real home. Falling in love with Leo is out of Adrik's control. There is no one else for Adrik, but he's not sure Leo can say the same.

Even though Adrik is way too young for Leo, and Leo was Adrik's guardian for six months before he turned eighteen, Leo can't help the way he feels. Adrik is twenty now. He has come a long way from the mess he was when Leo rescued him from a nightmare. Leo isn't sure he has come far enough, though. Adrik needs to have time to look at his options, and Leo is prepared to give him that time, no matter how much it hurts.

Neither Adrik nor Leo are looking anywhere else but at each other. Hopefully, they can figure that out before they ruin everything.

PROLOGUE

ADRIK'S STORY was so hard to write for many personal reasons. His story is ugly and there was no avoiding telling it so you could better understand him. I try to always warn people about possible triggers. This book is full of them, but it's so important for survivors to have a voice.

ONE

IT WAS a cabin in the middle of nowhere. His boss, Zander, had warned Adrik it would be, but he hadn't realized how far from civilization he would be on this trip to question a retired hitman. Adrik had thought he was brave enough for this. That enough time had passed. Until he saw the cabin, and the seclusion set in, that is. Each breath Adrik took came harder than the last. He was drowning on dry land. Every place he looked, Adrik saw the past. Adrik saw the face of the man who had destroyed him.

"Holy shit. Put your head between your knees."

Adrik found himself staring at the floorboard of Leo's Cadillac Escalade as Leo shoved his head down. He sucked air and detached from himself by staring at the black fibers beneath his feet. This floor was real. The trees surrounding the vehicle weren't the same as the ones in North Dakota. He wasn't trapped in the middle of nowhere with no escape. Leo was there. He was in a car. They could leave at any time. Adrik took another breath. His teeth chattered. He clamped his jaw shut and counted backward from a hundred in his head. Leo spoke in low tones, but Adrik couldn't hear a word over his own heartbeat.

It had been two and a half years since Leo had come to his rescue. Two and a half long years since he had been held against his will in the mountains. Nine hundred and twelve days since William Brantley. Just the thought of the name sent him spiraling. The burning sensation behind his eyes and nose pissed him off. He wasn't weak. Adrik was angry. This sick feeling that hit without warning and consumed his mind was a plague upon his life, reminding Adrik he would never be normal.

"That's it. We're going back to the hotel. You can't do this."

"I can do this," Adrik growled. As he geared up to fight, a light tapping on his window sent his heart rate back into overtime. Adrik shot upward. His gaze snapped to the window. No doubt he looked as crazed as he felt as he stared at the slender dark-haired man who waited to be acknowledged. His light-colored eyes were emotionless. He was gorgeous and terrifying in a way Adrik couldn't explain—like he had no soul. Yet Adrik found himself lowering his window. There was an odd sense of comfort in the man's emptiness.

"Adrik."

The thick Russian accent sounded so much like home that Adrik took his first clear breath since the isolation took hold. "Dmitry?"

Dmitry dipped his chin slightly. "I am who you came to see, no?"

Adrik couldn't hide his surprise. "You know me?"

The contract killer Zander had sent Adrik to see stared at him now with zero emotion, and it was freeing. "I know all the lost ones." His gaze moved past Adrik, locking on Leo for a moment before sliding back Adrik's way. "You may ask your questions, but your man must stay behind."

"He isn't my man," Adrik said automatically. It didn't matter. He had no clue why he argued. The words simply popped from his mouth.

Dmitry's gaze slid Leo's way once more before landing on Adrik again. "I'm not the one you need to convince. We should go inside. This location will not be good for your sanity, I would think."

Adrik didn't hesitate to exit the SUV. He knew Leo. If Adrik moved too slow, he would drive away to keep Adrik safe. Leo was overprotective like that. Dmitry kept a safe distance from Adrik. Adrik didn't for a second believe the space between them was for Dmitry's protection. After all, Dmitry Salko had taken out the entire Conti family, the same mafia family who had ruled the west coast for years, in a single night and walked away. No, it was Adrik's sanity he hoped to shield. That seemed an oddly kind gesture from a professional killer, even a retired one.

"This place is nothing like North Dakota." Adrik looked over at the comment. Dmitry kept his hands clasped behind his back as they headed toward the cabin. His gaze stayed locked ahead. Dmitry never looked his way. "It's mostly desert land here, once you get through our little patch of woods. There's also another house less than a mile away. You can leave any time you like."

It was the strangest conversation Adrik ever had. Dmitry was trying to keep him calm, ensuring him there were people around who could help if he ran. It worked. Adrik felt fine. Safe. It was funny

how the deadliest of people always made him feel
secure.

———

WHILE CHEWING THE SIDE OF HIS FINGERNAIL,
Leo stared at the front door of the cabin. His eyes
burned from not blinking. Adrik had disappeared
inside over an hour ago. Too many times to count,
Leo grabbed the door handle and fought the urge to
go after him. Adrik was his responsibility. Leo
wouldn't let anyone harm him. Never again.

Over forty years ago, a young Gio Conti made
his first visit to Russia. On that trip, he witnessed his
first street fight between a pair of teenagers. It had
been brutal, ending with one kid dead and the other
victorious. The savagery spoke to him on a sick level,
feeding a perversion he had somehow managed to
keep hidden until then. From that one moment
sprang a million tiny and unthinkable events. Gio
had begun filtering Russian children into the US.
Some were pitted against one another in what
amounted to underground human cock fights. The
rest were sold to the highest-bidding pervert for
whatever purpose they chose. Adrik was one of the
latter. Leo had found him and saved him, but there

were countless more out there. Leo and Adrik were two of the people trying to find the rest. Now Adrik was alone inside the home of the man who'd killed Gio Conti—a hitman by the name of Dmitry Salko. It was believed Dmitry had a list of Gio's victims. They needed that information. Since Adrik's name was on that list, he was the best person to ask for a copy. Leo recognized that on an intellectual level, but he was dying on the inside while waiting and praying Adrik wouldn't be hurt again in Gio's name.

The passenger side door opened, startling Leo so much, he jumped. He had no clue how Adrik had left the cabin without Leo seeing.

With his gaze averted, Adrik held out a thumb drive. His hand shook. "Names, addresses, and birthdates of every victim connected to the Conti family."

"Holy shit." Leo's gaze slid from the flash drive to Adrik's face. His eyes and nose were red. Leo's heart twisted. "You're the bravest person I've ever met."

Adrik finally met his stare. He looked hopeful— like he lived for Leo's praise. There was something else in his stare too, something Leo had noticed growing every day. Something Leo desperately wanted to believe was true. "We should probably go before he changes his mind."

Leo shook off his distraction. "Good call." Leo put the SUV in reverse while he still could. They would have all the time in the world to talk about what they wanted later, if they lived through this.

ADRIK CLUTCHED THE FLASH DRIVE TO HIS stomach and stared at nothing. He had done it. Their little vigilante group had been searching for this list of names since before Adrik had been rescued and allowed to join the fight. Adrik had gone from victim to possible savior in one conversation. Him. The weakest link. His insides shook, and he felt weaker than he had in months, but his feelings didn't matter. There were people just like him all over the US. They needed to be saved—like he had been. Adrik's gaze slid Leo's way. Leo kept switching his attention from the road to the mirrors, ensuring they weren't followed—the same as he had done the day he had rescued Adrik. Adrik loved him. It was a bit of a sickness at this point. Everything Adrik did, every new stride he made, it was all for Leo.

Leo glanced over, catching him staring. He winked before going back to watching the road. Adrik swore his heart skipped three beats. It was possible he suffered from a little hero worship when it came to Leo. If so, Adrik didn't care. For the past two and a half years, Leo had been his life. His safe place. Adrik didn't want anything to change.

"I think we should find a hotel and stay the night."

Adrik didn't really want to stay the night, but Leo had made the eight-hour drive that could have been a one-hour flight if Adrik hadn't been scared of flying. He couldn't ask Leo to make the trip in reverse again today. "That's fine. Whatever you need to do."

Leo leaned his way. Adrik immediately clutched Leo's arm and buried his face against it. He inhaled. Leo was his home. The pressure in his chest eased.

"I'm starving. We should get something to eat first."

Adrik nodded against Leo's arm. He knew Leo's chipper voice was for him. Leo was trying to diffuse an ugly setback before it happened. "That sounds good. I'm hungry too." It was a lie, but he felt the way Leo relaxed. Adrik sucked in another breath—like pulling some of Leo's life force into his body and shoring up his weak spots. It always worked. Adrik straightened his spine. He went on the hunt for his laptop. "I should probably send this list to Zander before there's any chance of losing it." He flipped open his laptop and plugged in the flash drive, staying focused on his task. This was his job. Adrik had willingly chosen this to save people like him. He could have taken the money Zander had freely offered him to make up for Gio destroying him, but he needed this—work that gave him purpose. This was the first day it didn't feel like a pity job. He had been the one to have the biggest break in Zander's hunt for Gio's sins. Leo was a cop. Another team member was an ex detective. They had tons of experience between them, but it was Adrik who had done the impossible. A smile tugged at his lips as he used his phone to set up a secure connection and copied the list. Once Adrik hit send, fresh air filled his lungs. He had proven himself to have value. Adrik wasn't simply a charity case any longer. People's lives would change for the better because of him. Adrik stared at Leo's profile. He was a step closer to being good enough to go after what he wanted the most—Leo.

TWO

IT HAD BEEN hell waiting for Adrik to fall asleep so he could sneak away. Leo prayed Adrik didn't wake up before he could get back. Adrik would likely freak if he found himself alone in a hotel with no idea where Leo had gone. Adrik might think he had been abandoned. Leo couldn't have that. He could have driven home tonight. No doubt Adrik would feel a hell of a lot better once he was surrounded by the familiar, but Leo couldn't leave. Not yet. He had to do this one more thing.

From his spot inside his SUV, Leo stared at the cabin, the same as he had done only hours earlier. It was a nice place. Since he had lived to return for a second visit, Leo appreciated the scenery a bit more this time. The cabin looked cozy—like a scene from a fairytale. It was possible a retired contract killer needed a fantasy home after a life of blood. It was equally easier to breathe this time around because Adrik wasn't factored into the mix. Two and a half years ago, Leo had burst into a different cabin, gun drawn, and determined to save a kid. He had found eerily light gray eyes watching him instead. Adrik had been six months away from eighteen. He had been sold at six and held against his will through all those years. They could have given him money and let him go. Leo couldn't. He had seen Adrik needed a lot more than money could buy. So, Leo had taken him in.

In the past two and a half years, everything had changed about Adrik. The starved and beaten teenager Leo had given a home to was now a skinny but grown man. He had taken to computers like a fish to water and several doctor appointments had him on the road to good health. William Bingham had kept a private doctor on call for Adrik. That doctor had kept Adrik alive, but not much else. Adrik needed glasses and shots. Antibiotics and IV bags of vitamins. Lots of food and bones reset. He had endured more than Leo could know, and that was the problem. Leo needed to know.

Only two people, other than Adrik, knew what

went down in that cabin of horrors for twelve years—William Bingham and the killer who lived in this cabin. William was dead, thanks to Zander's personal exterminator—Justice Alexandrov. The man was aptly named. He doled out the justice needed where the system failed. But that left only one person for Leo to question who could endure telling the story—Dmitry.

He hated sneaking away from the hotel while Adrik slept, but he had to know. With nothing else for it, Leo slipped from the SUV and headed for the door. He swiped his palms on his jeans as he cleared the porch. If Dmitry let him live, Leo wasn't sure where he would start. All Leo knew was he had to know what Adrik survived, because Leo was so sickeningly in love with Adrik, he couldn't function, but he needed to know how to make Adrik whole.

"It took you longer to show than I expected."

Leo jumped. His heart leapt into his throat. He spun, finding a calm-looking Dmitry behind him. His hands were shoved in his pockets and he leaned against the porch railing as if he had been there waiting all along. It was possible he had been, and Leo had walked right by him. Dmitry was like a ghost.

Leo patted his chest, trying to slow his heart. "You were expecting me?"

Dmitry dipped his chin. "You love Adrik. I knew you'd be back, wanting to know everything. If it were my Jozsua, I would be the same."

"Jozsua is your husband, right?" Leo was buying time, still trying to calm himself from being startled.

"He is. You should sit. Jozsua is trying to get our very willful toddler to go to sleep. Plus, we should leave this ugliness outside, don't you think?"

Leo was a little concerned he might not be allowed to leave here at all with all the details Dmitry freely gave him about his life, but he still moved to one of the porch's nearby rocking chairs and sat. It was too late to back down now. Once his ass hit the seat, Leo's mouth ran away from his brain.

"He doesn't talk to me and I don't know what to ask. The way he looked when he left here today, I get the feeling he talked to you."

A loud sigh filled the air as Dmitry lowered himself into the chair beside Leo. "That's only because I already knew most of it and I too was raised by monsters." Dmitry glanced over. "You were not. He won't want you to know what you've never been exposed to. You come from a good and loving

15

family, according to Adrik. He doesn't want you to know what it's like to be him."

Without thought, Leo snorted. "I've worked the sex crimes division for ten years. There are not many horrors I haven't seen."

"Seen," Dmitry mocked, sounding absent and looking away again. "Seeing is nothing. You absolutely cannot know what you don't know, and you don't know what it's like to live every day in the clutches of evil. When you're a survivor, everyone thinks you're strong. Truthfully, you're just so broken, you can no longer mimic the emotions people perceive as weak. But, unlike Adrik, I think you need to know what his life has been like. You look the type to stick around. For his sake, you should know what to expect."

Leo nodded while holding his tongue. He didn't want to interrupt and lose this chance. Leo had already stuck around for over two years, and he wasn't going anywhere, but there was a part of Adrik that Leo couldn't reach.

Dmitry stared straight ahead as if not truly seeing a thing except his thoughts. "As you know, Adrik was one of the children brought to this country and sold by Gio. But William Brantley was no typical buyer. He was raised in an extremely wealthy family that spoiled him beyond most people's imagination. When the day came that he was caught doing something heinous—"

"What was he caught doing?" Leo hated to interrupt, but he needed the full story, and he could take it. It was his job.

Dmitry shrugged. "I don't know. The information I gathered only said he'd done something so horrible, his family couldn't look the other way. But I can tell you that he had a very young sibling who died around the same time, so take what you will from that." Damn. That painted an ugly picture Leo didn't want, but he had asked for it.

"Anyhow," Dmitry said, moving on. "His parents decided to get him help. So, for many years, he was in a rehabilitation program that kept him medically castrated. If it's any consolation at all, which really it shouldn't be, he continued the medication for the rest of his life. He didn't like himself. William knew he had a sickness inside him, but he couldn't stay away from children. He went to many of Gio's sales and patted himself on the back when he left empty-handed. Then he saw Adrik." A sick feeling of dread overcame Leo, but he had to hear the whole of it. Dmitry met his stare, looking even darker than he had when Leo saw him the first time. "William took one look at Adrik and swore it was love. He would've paid any price to have him. William thought, if he could just keep Adrik, and stay on his meds, then Adrik would be like a pet. But his love really was a sickness, and he was eaten alive with need. Adrik was his most prized possession. Yet his presence was a constant torment, but William was also fiercely possessive. He was scared of getting caught and having Adrik taken away. That's why he took Adrik to the mountains and kept him hidden from the world. Adrik lived a nightmare in those woods. He couldn't run away. The place was too far from civilization. All Adrik had was twenty-four-seven access to the crazed William channel and whatever mood he was in that day. The thing is, as much as William loved Adrik, he also hated him. He blamed Adrik for making him love him—like Adrik had cast a spell over him. Adrik never knew which version of William he would get. He was trapped between the man's twisted love and sick hate. So William might spend one day torturing Adrik, doing his best to kill him. The next day, guilt would set in. He would spend the day apologizing, begging for forgiveness, petting Adrik, and pleasuring him. Then a different guilt would set in and he would be back to beating him. The fact that Adrik has any sanity left at all is a miracle." Dmitry held Leo's stare. Leo couldn't look away no matter how much Dmitry's story broke him. Those eerie light-colored eyes; they were familiar to Leo for some reason he couldn't place. "I know that you love him, but that's not enough. Adrik has been taught that love is an ugly thing that hurts."

"He's getting counseling. I never let him miss a session."

Dmitry shook his head. "That's not enough. He needs you to love him like he's whole, but you can never forget that he's not. If there's even the slightest chance that you can't handle his worst, you should leave him alone. He is like holding a butterfly. You have to let him choose to land in your hand. If you close your fist around him, you'll crush him. He needs your love to be free of guilt and control. Your love has to be pure and beautiful or he won't survive it."

Leo nodded. He knew Dmitry was right. An odd thought hit Leo. He couldn't keep it to himself. "You know, if I'd met you anywhere else, no one could convince me you've killed anyone."

Dmitry leaned closer. The slight smile that touched his lips chilled Leo's blood. "That's exactly why you would never see me coming."

Okay. He had stayed too long. In a show of

nerves, Leo slapped his knees and stood. "Well, I guess I'd better get back to Adrik. I don't like leaving him alone too long in new places. And you probably need to help your husband."

A low chuckle rumbled from Dmitry, as if he saw Leo's running for what it was. "Yes. Your Adrik is probably waiting. Oh, and Leopold, you should forget my address. I haven't visited California in a long time, but I'm not opposed to checking out Conrado Lane."

First off, no one knew his name was Leopold. Most people assumed Leo was short for Leonard. The mention of his address was even worse. Dmitry had done his homework and Leo didn't doubt for a second the man could make him disappear.

"You won't see me again."

"I know." The confidence in Dmitry's claim wasn't misplaced.

With a final nod, Leo headed back to his SUV. He kept his pace steady and didn't look back, no matter how badly he wanted to turn his head. Leo wouldn't be back. He had already learned what he had come here to hear. Adrik needed him. He would do his best.

Every light was on inside the room as Leo pulled into the parking spot outside. Leo's heart raced in his chest. He rushed to the door. It took three tries to get his hotel keycard to scan. Loud cursing rang in his head. He didn't take a steady breath until he set eyes on Adrik. In the same t-shirt and boxer briefs he had worn to bed, Adrik sat in the exact spot he had been sleeping in when Leo left. There was a hint of wild in his eyes—like he was a few minutes shy of completely coming apart.

"You disappeared."

The way Adrik sat with his knees to his chest and his arms wrapped around his knees—like holding himself—he made Leo wish he could be the one to hold him. He probably shouldn't feel this way about Adrik. Leo couldn't stop. He tried acting like leaving Adrik alone in a strange hotel was nothing out of the ordinary.

"I couldn't sleep."

Adrik chewed his bottom lip.

Leo fought the urge to cross the room and kiss him. He needed to fix scaring him shitless. "I didn't mean to wake you."

"You didn't. Normally, a hurricane wouldn't disturb me, but I forgot to bring that prescription they gave me to take at bedtime, and I can't sleep without it."

Leo gave in and crossed the room. He sat on the

end of Adrik's bed, keeping a safe distance between them in case Adrik wasn't in the right mindset to be touched. "You should've said something before I left. I could've found something for us to do together until you get tired."

Adrik's gaze dropped to his knees. "No. It's fine. I thought you might be sneaking away to find something to do with... other people," he finished, sounding unsure. Leo wondered what he had wanted to say before choosing to say "other people."

Leo infused as much humor as he could in his voice, trying to lighten Adrik's mood. "No. What? Are you kidding me? I just drove around aimlessly, hoping I'd get sleepy. You're the most fun person I know. There's no one I'd rather hang out with than you."

A slight smile passed over Adrik's lips. A blush touched his cheeks, but he still didn't look Leo's way. "You don't have to say that. I know I'm not exciting."

The laughter died in Leo's tone. "That's not true at all. I find you very exciting."

Adrik's gaze lifted to his. For a moment, Adrik simply held his stare. Heat grew between them. It was always like this with them. Leo didn't know how to stop. Adrik licked his lips, looking suddenly nervous. "Can I ask you something?"

Leo didn't hesitate. "Of course."

Adrik shook his head. "Never mind. It's stupid."

"You're never stupid. Ask away."

"No." Adrik shifted, looking uncomfortable. He found the edge of his blankets and tugged them upward, covering himself. "It's awkward and embarrassing and I just rather not," he said, settling onto his side.

Leo moved to his bed and turned down the covers. "All right. Just so you know, I'm right here. You can ask me anything. I'm not bothered." He kept his focus on the task of taking off his shirt and toeing off his shoes. Leo hoped, if he didn't look at Adrik, Adrik would relax. He stripped down to his underwear. When he turned and sat, Adrik was watching him. Leo took his time getting under the covers. He needed Adrik to see he wasn't uncomfortable.

"Is there someone you go to?" Adrik asked really fast like ripping off a bandage. He took an audible breath. "Like when I'm not around," Adrik added, as if that cleared up anything.

Leo got the gist of Adrik's question but wanted to be crystal clear before answering. "How do you mean? Like, am I dating anyone?"

Adrik shook his head again. "Never mind. Forget I asked. Like I said, I'm being stupid."

Leo wished he would stop saying that. "I'm not dating anyone." He wasn't letting this go and having Adrik thinking they couldn't talk about anything he wanted to discuss.

"I guess I knew that. In a way." Adrik sounded sad for some reason. He didn't make Leo ask. "I mean, you work all the time, and anytime you're actually off, you're taking care of me. Really, what I meant was, you have like... needs. Jesus." His face was solid red. "Surely there's someone you go to for that."

"There used to be," Leo said, determined to make Adrik understand that nothing was off limits between them. Adrik couldn't make him uncomfortable. "A couple of years ago, but no. Not for a long time."

"Why?"

Since Adrik was still open to discussing this, Leo kept answering his questions. He chuckled. "At the risk of sounding lame, I'm not a booty call kind of guy. I like relationships. Nights in front of the TV, looking like hell, and eating snacks. I love it when you're so comfortable with someone that you don't worry about anything, because you know they love you no matter what. Not the way you look or what you can do for them, just you." He shrugged. "If I can't have that, then I guess I don't want anything."

Adrik stared at nothing and chewed his bottom lip. Leo watched him until his eyelids grew heavy. The moment he almost gave in to sleep, Adrik chuckled. "I just realized. You described us."

"I suppose I did," Leo said, sounding half asleep even to his ears. He closed his eyes.

"Leo?"

"Hmm?"

"Is it okay if I sleep with you? I don't like this town."

He should've known not to leave Adrik alone in this place that reminded him too much of the past. Leo immediately scooted over, making room for Adrik. He lifted the covers and Adrik scrambled from his bed to Leo's. Despite Adrik's closeness, Leo still tried dozing off. He was always comfortable with Adrik.

"Leo?" This time, it was a whisper.

"Hmm?"

"If I ask to do something else, would you try not to laugh at me?"

Leo peeked one eye open to find Adrik looking nervous as hell. "Of course."

"Could I—maybe—try kissing you?" Adrik looked horrified and defeated all at once—like he couldn't decide if he should bite off his tongue or go ahead and die.

Leo's body didn't care that Adrik was embarrassed. It stirred to life. He had been quietly starving for Adrik for a long time. "Yes."

Adrik's gaze shot to Leo's face. He moved closer. His fingers caressed Leo's ribs as Adrik visibly worked up the courage to do as he wanted. He leaned closer. His warm breath fanned across Leo's face. Leo's eyes fell closed as Adrik's lips lightly brushed his. He quickly backed away and settled on his side with his chin down, hiding his expression. "Sorry. I shouldn't have put you in this position. You probably think I'm a complete head case."

"Adrik." Leo kept his voice soft, trying not to scare Adrik away. "Please look at me?" Adrik lifted his chin, but his eyes still didn't quite meet Leo's stare. "Would it be okay if I kissed you back?"

Adrik looked as if he held his breath. He didn't blink. "Yes."

Leo moved slow. The last thing he wanted was to scare Adrik. Adrik lived with him. Leo was all he had. If Adrik freaked, he could end up anywhere. Leo wouldn't be allowed to watch him any longer.

That would kill him. This time, when their lips met, Leo felt Adrik's breath catch. He didn't move. Adrik held perfectly still. Leo worried Adrik would strain a muscle in his attempt to remain completely stiff. Then, Leo opened his mouth over Adrik's bottom lip. Adrik gasped. His palms landed on Leo's chest, as if he might push Leo away. Leo leaned away, scared as hell of spooking Adrik.

"I can stop." Before the final word fully left his lips, Adrik claimed his mouth. Hot and hard. Their teeth bumped in Adrik's attack.

He immediately pulled away, looking upset. "I'm sorry." He touched Leo's lips as if patting them down and checking for signs of injury. "I'm such an idiot. I don't know what I'm doing."

Leo kissed Adrik's fingertips. "Stop, sweetie. It's okay. Just stop. Come here," Leo said, tugging Adrik close. This wasn't going well. Leo knew if he didn't find a way to make this next kiss perfect, Adrik would never try again. With Adrik on his back and Leo's leg tossed over him so he could control their pace, Leo lowered his head and kissed him. This time, he didn't hold back. Instead, he chose to overwhelm Adrik. He immediately delved inside, stroking Adrik's tongue with his. Adrik's kiss was sweet and undeniably timid. His fingers fluttered to

27

Leo's side before immediately disappearing, as if he was afraid to touch Leo too much. Every stroke of his tongue felt questioning—like Adrik thought he did something wrong and waited between each stroke for chastisement. Leo didn't press. He already knew they would share this kiss and go to sleep. Adrik might never be whole enough for more. The crazy thing was, Leo didn't care. Ten years ago, he would have scoffed at the idea of being with someone who couldn't have a sexual relationship with him. Love was a funny thing, though. Leo would rather have Adrik and no sexual contact than the hottest porn star around. Adrik was everything.

Leo spent a moment doing nothing more than lightly sucking Adrik's bottom lip, before kissing his cheek and settling back down beside him. "Good night, baby."

Adrik took a ragged-sounding breath. "Good night."

With his eyes squeezed shut, Leo tried to will his body into calming. His lust meant nothing. It was just that—desire. Adrik's mental stability meant more than Leo's natural reaction to stimulus.

"Leo?" Adrik whispered.

"Yeah."

"I love you."

Leo's body relaxed. They had exchanged I love yous for the first time over a year ago. Now, they told each other all the time. Sometimes, Leo wasn't even sure what kind of love they shared. All he knew was —it was real. "I love you too."

"I wish..." Adrik paused, as if scared to continue. Leo waited him out. Finally, Adrik took a sharp breath and spoke fast. "I wish I was who you came to when you need more."

Leo's eyes opened. He tried not to appear as shocked as he was as he stared at Adrik. His mind raced for the right words. The last thing Leo wanted was to sound condescending or controlling, but Adrik wasn't ready for that. He had barely endured a kiss. "I wish you understood you're the only person I want. You don't have to worry I'm going elsewhere, but I also don't want you to rush on my account. Whenever you're ready for me, I'm not going anywhere."

To his surprise, Adrik sniffed, and a tear fell from the corner of his eye. Adrik never turned his face Leo's way. He kept his gaze locked on the ceiling. He sucked in a stuttered sounding breath. Leo worried Adrik was on the edge of completely coming apart. He held Adrik tighter.

Leo stroked Adrik's stomach. "It's okay, sweetie.

You can say absolutely anything to me. Nothing is off limits. I'll never laugh at you or think less of you. You're free and safe here."

He visibly swallowed, making Leo's throat hurt at the sight. "I have needs too and I hate myself for it," Adrik said, crying harder. He sniffed again. "I don't like that I can't control it—like I've never been able to control it, even when I didn't want to do certain..."

Jesus. Leo's chest hurt and his eyes burned. He got it. William might have been chemically castrated, but he had still gotten a sick thrill from making Adrik come. Everything about sex and love that should be healthy and normal was a distorted mess in Adrik's head. He knew therapists were working with Adrik, but there was only so much they could do. Everyone could tell him certain things were completely normal, but Adrik would never know he wasn't doing anything wrong until someone showed him.

"Adrik." Even Leo heard the longing in his voice. He couldn't control it. Leo ached for Adrik to feel whole. "You're the one in charge of your life now. I'm where you can go when you feel anything at all. You should use me."

Adrik finally turned his head. His eyes and nose were red, and he was still beautiful. "What?"

Leo gave him a sharp nod. He didn't know how else to help. "Anytime you feel anything at all, bring it to me. I want your anger, happiness, sadness, and whatever you've got. I'm at your mercy. Whatever you want, do it. You have my consent."

"Really?" Adrik sounded stronger.

Leo nodded. "When I say that I love you, I mean it. I'm not just saying the words. I really do love you. That means I need your happiness like I need air. Give me your worst. I can take it."

Adrik sniffed, obviously still trying to get his emotions under control. "What if I touch you and then I freak out? I don't want to make you angry."

A smile tugged at Leo's lips. "Have I ever been mad at you?"

"Yes," Adrik said without missing a beat.

That was true. "Let me rephrase that. Have I ever been mad at you and you felt threatened by my anger?"

Adrik seemed to think it over this time. "No. I've screamed at you many times."

A chuckle sneaked out at Adrik's claim. There had been many yelling matches between them in the past couple of years. "You're sexy as hell when you're angry."

A blush exploded across Adrik's cheeks. "You

make me feel things in my chest," Adrik said, making Leo's throat swell with emotion. Adrik's voice dropped to a whisper, as if his bravery was failing. "I like it when you look at me." Goddamn. Leo was hard to the point of misery. No one had ever turned him on so quickly with only their words. "You look like you'd do anything I ask."

"I would," Leo said without hesitation.

Adrik rolled to his side, facing Leo. His fingertips brushed down Leo's ribs. Leo fought the urge to squirm. Not only did the move tickle, but he was so aroused, his skin was on fire. Adrik licked his lips, looking nervous. His hand moved lower, skimming Leo's hip. "I like looking at you too," Adrik whispered like revealing a dirty secret. "You're very pretty."

Leo bit the inside of his cheek to hide his humor over the statement. No one had ever referred to him as pretty before.

Adrik lightly stroked Leo's erection through his underwear, as if ready to jump away. "Don't touch me, okay?" The whispered demand broke Leo's heart. Not because he wasn't allowed to touch Adrik, but because Adrik still feared being touched.

"I won't."

At his promise, Adrik slipped his hand inside

Leo's underwear. Leo almost came right then. Adrik's touch was so light and unsure, but Leo had never expected to feel Adrik like this. He sucked in a breath and tried holding still as Adrik massaged him. Adrik's gaze never wavered from Leo's face—like he was fascinated by Leo's reactions. Leo's lips parted on a gasp he couldn't hold. Adrik kept petting him. His touch never firmed or moved faster. Leo didn't think Adrik meant to torture him, but he was. Every muscle was taut as he crept closer to orgasm. Leo took turns holding his breath and gasping for air. He wondered if his brain would snap as he fought not to move or touch Adrik. His entire body spasmed as release hit. The desire to kiss Adrik and bring him the same pleasure was almost maddening. His skin itched with a need to do so many things he wasn't allowed to do.

"So pretty," Adrik whispered. He shifted positions and pressed his lips to Leo's. Leo held still, afraid to move when he had promised he wouldn't touch Adrik. "Leo." There was so much longing in that one word that Leo's skin felt too tight. Even with his mind freshly blown, Leo still needed more. He needed Adrik to feel the same.

"Tell me how to fix it, baby."

Adrik moved restlessly against him. "I don't

know." He buried his face in the crook of Leo's neck. "I want you to be different. Maybe we could practice... I don't know." He sucked an audible breath against Leo's skin. "You can touch me."

Leo took it in the gut. He stroked Adrik's back, hoping to soothe him while Leo's mind raced. "Do you trust me?"

Adrik nodded. "It's my mind I don't trust."

"I believe in you enough for the both of us." He rolled, gently bringing Adrik along with him until Adrik was draped over him like a blanket. Cum soaked his underwear in a very uncomfortable way, but this was more important. He kissed Adrik's head. "You should use me." He rotated his hips, rocking into Adrik's erection and leaving no doubt what he meant.

For a moment, Adrik didn't move and Leo couldn't breathe under the pressure. The last thing he wanted was to trigger Adrik. Then Adrik shifted. He straddled Leo's body. Adrik didn't lift his head. He kept his forehead pressed to Leo's chest as he rocked forward, using the friction between their bodies to reach for release. Adrik moved hesitantly at first. His breathing turned ragged and his shoulders heaved. Leo couldn't as much as blink. He couldn't explain the thousand emotions raging through him.

Leo needed for Adrik to explode—lose himself. He needed to be the one Adrik shared that first willing orgasm with.

Adrik kissed his chest. His thrusts turned frantic. He visibly fought with himself, needing more. His teeth sank into Leo's skin. A moan escaped Leo before he could stop it. Adrik cried out. He tried to hide the way he shook as he gasped against Leo's chest. Leo's eyes burned. He had never been more moved by anyone in his life. Even once Adrik's breathing returned to normal, he still didn't move or lift his chin. Worry ate at Leo. Adrik didn't make a single sound. It was frightening as hell. He hoped Adrik wasn't about to fall apart.

Leo rubbed Adrik's back. He kept his voice soft. "Are you okay, baby? I've got you."

Adrik kept his face pressed to Leo's chest. "I'm just really embarrassed right now." His voice came out muffled.

Leo bit the inside of his cheek to keep from laughing. Adrik was really adorable sometimes. Leo hadn't realized how sexy awkwardness was until Adrik. He put every practiced man Leo had ever met to shame. "Imagine how I feel. You stared at me while I came."

At his claim, Adrik met his stare. He looked

endearingly disgruntled. "Nothing embarrasses you. You're shameless."

That was true. Still, he didn't have to let Adrik get away with saying it. "I mean, how would you know? Maybe I'll be scarred for life now."

Adrik pinched his side. It was worth it to see Adrik come back to life. He rubbed the spot where Adrik had bruised him. "Okay, okay. I'm shameless, but wow. That was sexy. I want to watch you come unglued again." A blush exploded across Adrik's face. He tried hiding again, but Leo cupped his cheeks before he could get away. He held Adrik's stare. "You're beautiful. If you want to hide, maybe you could kiss me. I always keep my eyes closed for that." Adrik's flushed cheeks and open love punched Leo in the chest. Adrik didn't possess an ounce of artifice and it was like breathing fresh air for someone like Leo. Leo worked both sides of the law, bringing down the worst sex offenders in the world. Adrik was innocence personified. Leo had to protect him. He couldn't help but love him. "Please?"

At his plea, Adrik transformed into a warrior. His bravery surged to the surface. He kissed Leo. This time, there wasn't any nervousness in Adrik's touch. He didn't flinch from Leo's touch as Leo deepened their kiss. Leo didn't stop until he felt

Adrik's body completely melt. The dazed expression Adrik wore was the most beautiful thing Leo had ever seen.

"You leave me speechless."

Adrik blinked at the claim—like coming back to himself. He still didn't look away, even as he visibly swallowed. "Maybe we could practice this touching thing and I won't be so horrified next time."

It was hard, but Leo kept a straight face. No way was he losing this chance. "I'd love that."

With a tiny nod, Adrik kissed him again, and Leo lost himself. Someday, Adrik would be whole. Leo would make sure of it. Even if he didn't get there, Leo would love him for the rest of his life. Adrik's life would be beautiful. Leo couldn't have it any other way.

THREE

FROM DAY ONE, Adrik had gone to the gym with Leo every day. Leo worked out. Adrik worked on his laptop while watching Leo on the sly. He had never thought about how intriguing it would be to watch another person's muscles flex. The way sweat rolled down Leo's body, making him shimmer, always made it a little harder for Adrik to breathe. Leo might be fifteen years older than Adrik, but he looked better than Adrik. Adrik had missed out on some crucial years of proper care. His body would always show it.

Leo was six-six and kept his head shaved bald. There was a tattoo of Lady Justice on Leo's left side and a scar up his knee from surgery years ago. His eyes were a shade of amber—like a tiger. Adrik could describe Leo to the tiniest detail, and—sometimes—

he worried Leo got sick of him always being under foot. Surely there was nothing sexy about a needy, fucked-up mess. Adrik knew he was a good fifty pounds underweight and walked funny from all the broken bones he had suffered. He was scared of everything, even though he tried not to be. Adrik wore glasses he couldn't see a damn thing without. He was awkward and pretty much useless in every way. In truth, Adrik had no idea why Leo kept him around. Pity, most likely.

"Get up and come join us," Legend yelled, trying to convince Adrik to learn how to box, the way he did every day while sparring with Leo.

Adrik assumed Legend had a real name, but he had never heard it. "No, thank you," Adrik said quietly, the way he did every day. He knew he should explain he had already been hit enough for one lifetime, but Adrik always left his answer at no.

Legend bounced around on his toes while pretending to land hits every place he could reach on Leo's body. "Come on, old man. Show Addy how it's done." Legend shuffled his feet, being ridiculous. "Make me hurt, Daddy."

Leo smiled at Legend's antics.

Adrik stared in half fascination and half debilitating jealousy. Legend was blond, tall, muscular, and all around perfect. He didn't wear glasses and his teeth were perfectly straight. Legend was flawless in a way Adrik would never achieve. That was bad enough. It wasn't fair for the man to also have a winning personality. Adrik did not want to notice the way Leo's eyes shone with happiness as he watched Legend dancing around. He dropped his gaze to his computer screen. His homework blurred. Adrik blinked. He was twenty and still trying to catch up to people five years younger. Some days, Adrik felt like giving up. Against his will, Adrik's gaze lifted again. Leo stared back at him. A wave of love washed over Adrik. Even if Leo chose Legend, Adrik didn't think he could let go. He definitely could never hate the man. Anyone with an ounce of sense wouldn't choose him.

Without a word, Adrik set his laptop aside and came to his feet. Leo never looked away as Adrik closed the distance between them.

Leo's mouth lifted in one corner. "I'm covered in sweat."

"I don't care." Adrik had never meant anything more. He snagged Leo's t-shirt and lured him down. Adrik went up on his toes and pressed his lips to Leo's. He felt more than heard Leo's hum. Adrik lightly sucked Leo's bottom lip before moving away. He didn't release Leo's shirt.

"I love you."

Happiness was restored at Leo's claim. "I love you too."

"I'll get in the shower."

Adrik nodded. "Whenever you're ready. I wasn't rushing you."

Leo dipped his head again and kissed the corner of Adrik's mouth. Adrik's heart swelled. It was like Leo was publicly choosing him. He tried not to blush or smile like an idiot as Leo walked away. Instead, Adrik kept his head down and moved back to his laptop. He stared at the screen again, seeing nothing. Before Adrik had time to react, the laptop disappeared from his lap and Legend pulled him to his feet. Adrik fought the immediate terror that washed over him.

"Okay. No one can see you. It's time for you to learn how to defend yourself."

Adrik sucked air, trying to make sense of Legend's words. "No." Even Adrik didn't know if he declined Legend's offer or his touch. Either way, he needed Legend to let go.

Legend's hold loosened on Adrik's wrists and turned into a caress. He stared down at Adrik with his heart in his eyes. "You're incredibly brave. I'm thoroughly put in my place after that kiss. Now let me teach you how to never let anyone physically hurt you."

He didn't want this, but Adrik couldn't find his voice again. Logically, he knew Legend was only a couple of years older than him, but his eyes looked ancient in that moment—like he saw more than Adrik liked.

"Leo would kill me if I did anything to harm you and I like being alive. Let me help," Legend cajoled when Adrik still hadn't found his tongue.

Adrik gave a sharp nod. Horror welled inside of him as he realized what he had done. The thing was, if he ever hoped to be seen as Leo's equal and as a real part of Zander's team, he needed to know how to defend himself.

Legend didn't show an ounce of triumph. "You're safe here. We'll talk through everything before we try each new move. That way, you'll always know what to expect. Okay?"

"Okay." Even to Adrik's ears, he sounded small. Some day he would be different. One day, he would make Leo proud. With that idea growing in his head, Adrik nodded. "Okay," he said again. This time, he heard the determination growing in his voice. He would be worthy of the man who had saved him.

WITH HIS HAIR STILL DRIPPING FROM HIS shower, Leo gathered his stuff. He only had about two more hours until he needed to be at work and he still had to drop Adrik off at his job. Two hours was plenty of time, except Leo wanted a few minutes alone with Adrik too. The way Adrik had been watching him this morning made Leo think Adrik might be open to practicing touches again. No way in hell was Leo missing that.

Leo's feet froze to the floor as Adrik came into view. Adrik stood in the center of the sparring mat while Legend taped his knuckles. Legend looked closely at Adrik's hand. Adrik pretended to punch him and Legend went down hard in an exaggerated knockout. Adrik's laughter could be heard across the room. Leo smiled at the sound. He didn't think he had ever seen Adrik this openly happy. Maybe it was due to Legend being a complete idiot, but Leo feared it had more to do with Legend being closer to Adrik in age. Not only did Adrik not have to fear being molested by an old man in Legend's company, Adrik had the freedom of spending time with someone who didn't know about his past. With Legend, Adrik could be a normal twenty-year-old.

Leo's smile fell. He loved Adrik. Maybe that meant he should set Adrik free. William's twisted love had kept Adrik prisoner. It was possible that seeing Leo as his hero and feeling like he owed everything to Leo held Adrik a different type of hostage. Leo wanted Adrik to choose his future. He wanted to know Adrik lived his best life—whether it included Leo or not. Leo's eyes fell closed. He took a breath and dug deep. When his eyes reopened, he pasted on a smile he didn't feel.

"Look at you."

Adrik blushed and dropped his gaze at Leo's arrival.

"He's awesome," Legend praised, jumping to his feet. "A natural born fighter."

"Legend is only being nice." Even though Adrik said the words to the mat, Leo heard the hint of pride. Adrik needed this more than he needed Leo. Leo could live with losing Adrik, as long as he knew Adrik was happy and whole.

"Hey, you should hang out with Legend and get some practice in," Leo suggested. "You can work from home later. I can come back and get you on my way to work in a couple of hours."

Legend cut in. "I can give him a ride to wherever later. If that's okay with Adrik, of course."

They were so close in age. Adrik needed that. He needed friends. Leo felt his heart crack. Maybe he had gotten a little too attached to being the center of Adrik's life. Maybe their time together was more for him, when it should be about Adrik. "What do you think, Adrik?"

Adrik's gaze lifted. He looked from Leo to Legend and back again. He didn't look scared at all. Leo couldn't get past it. "Um, sure. I mean, if you really don't mind, Legend."

"Mind?" Legend asked, flashing his usual bright and boyish smile. "I'd be honored. It's not often I get to show off my manliness under the guise of training."

Adrik blushed and shook his head at Legend's antics.

Leo wondered if he could do this. If he could walk away. Let go. "Do you want me to take your laptop home with me?"

Adrik's gaze slid toward the device. That another lifeline Adrik clung too hard to, escaping into technology. "That's probably a good idea. I won't have to keep an eye on it."

He was doing the right thing, Leo reminded himself. That wasn't always the easy path. "All right. Have fun, sweetie. Call me later."

"Okay."

With Adrik's promise to call, Leo gathered the laptop and headed for the door. He didn't look back. It was hard. He wanted to throw Adrik over his shoulder and run from the building, but that was the problem, wasn't it? That was exactly what Adrik had already survived once. Leo needed to be different. He had to be the hero.

THEY DIDN'T DO ENOUGH FOR ADRIK TO EVEN break a sweat. He mostly watched Legend goof off while occasionally showing him some self-defense moves. Still, Adrik had a surprisingly good time. Legend was like a big kid. It was refreshing and freeing.

"So, am I taking you home, work, or would you like to get some ice cream with me?"

"Ice cream? Doesn't that negate all the hard work you put in at the gym?"

Legend looked offended. "What's the point of spending all my time at the gym if I can't have ice cream? Plus, there's this place within walking distance that has all these candies and cookie doughs. It's like a kid's dream come true. Since we're walking there, that's another reason we don't have to feel guilty for eating as much as we want."

Adrik shook his head at Legend's antics, but he couldn't stop smiling. "Okay."

"Woot." Legend bounced on his toes like an overactive child.

He liked Legend more than he wanted to admit. It was impossible not to smile around him. As they made their way inside the ice cream shop, they chatted about nothing while Adrik tried hiding how overwhelmed he was by the creamery. It smelled amazing and there was so much to choose from, he didn't know where to start.

"They have edible cookie dough here?"

Legend glanced over, looking confused. "Yeah. They don't put egg in it, so it's completely safe to eat."

Adrik curled his nose. It seemed an odd thing to sell or eat. "Is it any good?"

"Are you joking? How have you never had cookie dough?"

"I don't know," Adrik said, keeping his face averted. "There's a lot I haven't done or tried."

"You're getting the chocolate chip cookie dough. That's a classic. I'll get the peanut butter and chocolate chunk. That way, you can try mine too. What else haven't you done that'll shock me?"

Adrik shrugged. "I don't know." He thought it over while they waited for their order. There were probably millions of things he hadn't tried that most people his age had already done hundreds of times. Adrik racked his brain. "I don't drive."

Legend shrugged. "That much I figured by Leo driving you around. Also, that's not all that unusual. Driving is expensive. It's getting harder and harder for young adults to afford cars."

The claim eased Adrik's embarrassment and loosened his tongue. "I've never ridden a bike or been on vacation." Adrik spaced out for a minute as his brain overloaded on the countless things he had missed. He had never been hugged by a parent or gone to school. Adrik wondered if Legend would think he was a freak.

"Even though I've always been an exercise freak, I don't like bikes either. In this town, you're likely to get killed if you tried biking anywhere." Legend paid for their food before Adrik could intervene. He handed Adrik his bowl. "As to vacations, I've never really been anywhere either. I was raised by a single mom and we were poor. We lived with my grandma." Legend picked out a table for them in the corner and kept talking. "My mom homeschooled me during the day and worked at night. Sometimes, during the summer, we'd go down to the Santa Monica pier. We'd ride all the rides and try all the fried foods before driving back home. I know Mom had to be exhausted, but she never complained." Legend took a bite of his cookie dough and stared at nothing. Adrik wondered if Legend was secretly unhappy. His gaze landed on Adrik again and his face brightened. "We should do that sometime—drive down to the pier. It's a blast."

Adrik didn't know anything about this pier, but he could Google it later. "Sounds fun." Another thought hit Adrik. "You know, I haven't thought to ask what you do. Wouldn't you have to miss work?"

Legend dropped his gaze to his food. He scooped out a spoonful and held it out to Adrik. "Try this." Adrik dutifully leaned forward and accepted the bite. Jesus. It was delicious. He was in sugar heaven. Legend struck while Adrik's mouth was full. "I'm an escort. So I'm pretty free most days except weekends." He said the words fast—like he was ashamed.

"That's delicious," Adrik said, pointing at the bowl. "I don't know what an escort is."

A sardonic-looking smile touched Legend's lips as he kept staring at his food. His dark blue gaze finally lifted. "I go on dates for money."

"Okay."

Legend shook his head. "That's it? Just okay?"

Confusion made Adrik slow to respond. "Yeah. That sounds completely terrifying to me, but I'm scared of everything." Adrik wanted to bite off his tongue. Instead, he kept talking. "But you're not like me. I imagine you're pretty popular." He smiled. "I would pay to go out with you."

"It's three thousand a night."

Adrik shoved some cookie dough in his mouth, hoping to hide his reaction. That was a lot of money for a date. The kind of money that came with expectations, he imagined. Since Adrik didn't know how to ask what Legend was expected to do for that much pay, he kept his mouth full.

Thankfully, Legend didn't seem to need him for this conversation. "I'd never expect you to pay me, of course. It's just that you asked, so... there you go.

That's what I do." He was back to sounding uncomfortable.

Adrik had been sold once. If anyone understood that came with a bit of shame, it was him. Except he hadn't been the one who profited from his pain and it wasn't at all the same. He felt out of his element. "I think you're amazing," Adrik said, finding his tongue. The claim came out sounding small but sincere. If there was anything Adrik understood, it was that sometimes everyone needed to hear they were liked for themselves and weren't defined by anything else.

Legend smiled and Adrik felt like it was the first genuine look he had ever gotten of the real Legend. Before he could dig for more, Legend turned the conversation his way. "What do you do?"

"I work in loss prevention for Luna Casino." He shrugged. "I just go over all the security footage and whatnot, looking for anything suspicious," Adrik said, sticking with the lie he had practiced many times. "That's actually how I met Leo."

Legend leaned closer. "That reminds me. What's the story with you two?"

Adrik fought the urge to squirm. "What do you mean?"

"Well, I mean, sometimes you two act like a couple

and other times you don't. Like, I get there's something between you, but it looks like you're—maybe—best friends, but with benefits. I can't really tell."

Even though he had never heard a friendship described as having benefits, Adrik thought it might be a decent description for them. "I suppose that's right."

A huge grin spread across Legend's face. "That's good to hear. So, like, you're free to see other people?"

Adrik's heart sank. "Yeah, I suppose if Leo wants to go out with you, then I can't stop him."

Legend blinked. "What? I'm not interested in going out with Leo."

For a moment, Adrik tried working that out in his head before giving up. "Then why all the questions?"

Legend snorted and shook his head. "Because I'm interested in you, dummy."

That didn't make sense. No one in their right mind would be interested in him, especially someone perfect like Legend. "But you're always dancing around and flirting with Leo," Adrik said, grasping at straws.

"No," Legend said with a laugh. "I'm showing

out for you. Wow. You'd think you'd never met anyone over-the-top conceited before."

Adrik felt the same way he did when faced with an impossible math equation. Nothing made sense. "But... why?"

Legend laughed harder. "You really are adorkable, aren't you?"

"I... what?"

"Can we go do something? I mean, would you spend the rest of the day with me?"

Adrik's confusion grew by the second, but he could see Legend was sincere. "Yes." They would never be more than friends, but he wasn't sure Leo considered himself more than a friend either. Relationships were confusing and hard work. Adrik felt like a goddamn idiot.

"I need to run by my place and change clothes first. Then, road trip. We'll have so much fun."

Legend was so engaging, Adrik couldn't help but get sucked in to his excitement. It was nice to feel young for once. Still, he wished Leo was there.

TEN O'CLOCK PASSED AND ADRIK STILL WASN'T

home. Leo tried his damnedest not to pace the floor like a complete psychopath. He had caved two hours earlier and texted Adrik, only to learn he had gone to Santa Monica with Legend. That was five hours away, for fuck's sake. Adrik was a grown man. He was allowed to go wherever he wanted. Goddamn it. There was a good chance Adrik wouldn't come home tonight. Where would he sleep? Legend didn't know Adrik's past. What if Adrik had a panic attack? He hadn't taken his meds with him. Fuck, Leo couldn't take this. He didn't have a choice. Leo didn't own Adrik. Adrik was his own person with thoughts, feelings, and... needs. Leo's gut twisted with jealousy. He was the one who was supposed to help Adrik with that aspect of his life. But maybe Legend was the better choice. Adrik wouldn't have to feel damaged. Leo needed a drink.

He headed for the kitchen. Time passed with no input from him as he stared inside the liquor cabinet. As his fingers wrapped around the neck of a bottle of Jack, someone knocked on the door. Leo snagged the bottle and carried it with him to the living room. His gaze moved toward his service weapon before dismissing it. It was no wonder Adrik was unhappy living with him. Leo was a paranoid bastard who had seen way too much in his life. At least one of them should be normal. Leo checked the peephole and blinked. Justice stood on the other side. He hadn't realized Justice even knew where he lived. They didn't have much to do with each other outside Leo's part-time job with Zander.

Leo opened the door. "Hey. What's up?"

Justice's gaze moved over his face before dropping to the bottle Leo held. Finally, he met Leo's stare again. "Not much. I came to talk to Adrik."

"He's not here, but come in. It's possible he'll be back any minute. He didn't really give me a time."

With a nod, Justice stepped inside. He didn't move, twitch, or inspect the room. Justice stood in place and waited to be invited to sit. He was a scary bastard.

Leo motioned in the general direction of the living room furniture. "Sit wherever you like." He waited until after Justice settled on the loveseat before continuing. "I know you came looking for Adrik, but is there anything I can help you with?" Leo asked as he sat across from him.

Justice shook his head. "I'm not sure. Do you know if Adrik had a look at that list Salko gave him before handing it off to Zander?"

Leo set his bottle on the coffee table and his elbows on his knees, giving Justice his full attention. Anything at all was better than focusing on the dark clouds brewing inside his mind. "I'm not sure. Is there a reason you're asking?"

Leo had never seen Justice look uncomfortable. He was seeing it now. Justice's gaze slid away. "I just think—maybe—he should have a look at it when he gets time."

"All right." Even Leo heard the question in his tone. "I'll talk to him about it when he gets home."

Justice swiped his palms on his pants. "You might want to have a look with him."

Now Leo was really curious. "Okay. I'm not sure if he still has a copy, but we'll take a look at it if he does." Leo cracked open his bottle. "Would you like a drink? Like I said, I don't know when Adrik will be home. He went with Legend to Santa Monica. Since all his meds are here, I assume he means to come home tonight."

For a moment, Justice stared at him in silence. He ignored Leo's offer for a drink. "Adrik is safe with Legend, but is Legend safe from you?"

Leo was determined to ride this out. He played the ignorance card. "Of course. They're close in age and Adrik needs friends." Fuck, even Leo heard the way he tried only to convince himself.

"You should keep the liquor for yourself. I have a feeling you need it."

Leo tossed the bottle's cap onto the table and sat back. The soft leather cushioned him but brought no comfort. He caved. "For real, Justice, I don't know what I'm doing. I'm trying hard here to do the right thing."

Justice didn't judge. Leo appreciated it more than he could say. "Adrik is young. He's more resilient than you think. But he's also seen evil most people are spared. Legend is not built to handle that. He's all charm and showy tricks. Adrik needs peace. He won't fall for the smiles."

As much as Leo wanted to hope, he also didn't know if Justice was right. Maybe Adrik needed light and laughter after all the years of sick rage. The liquor burned his throat as Leo took a huge swig without bothering with a glass. This was the first night he had been without Adrik in years. He hated it. Leo had no clue what to do with himself. He wasn't built to be alone anymore.

SPENDING THE DAY WITH LEGEND WAS LIKE A vacation from himself. Legend was obnoxious, conceited, and completely overwhelming. Adrik had laughed and smiled so much that his face and throat hurt. But Adrik was off balance with Legend and he missed Leo so much, his chest ached. Legend couldn't drive fast enough to get him home. Adrik fought the urge to leap from Legend's Charger and rush the door.

Instead, he measured each step. Legend kept pace with him. "This was fun."

It was. Even though Adrik was over it for the night, he hoped they got to do it again. "You're a unique soul," Adrik said for lack of anything else.

Legend turned and walked backward before stepping into Adrik's path. "Did you just call me a weirdo?"

Adrik snorted and shook his head. "You dig for praise too often for someone who doesn't need bolstering."

"Well, if I can't get compliments, I'll settle for kisses." That was all the warning Adrik got before Legend's mouth covered his.

Shock froze him in place for longer than he liked. It wasn't an unpleasant experience, but he wasn't Leo.

Adrik flattened his palms on Legend's chest. He gently pushed Legend away, cringing the whole way. The last thing Adrik wanted was to hurt Legend, but they couldn't be more than friends.

Legend pulled a face. "You really only want Leo, don't you?"

Adrik winced. "I'm sorry. Whether or not I'm the one for him, he's the one for me."

"It's not that I don't get it," Legend said, sounding defeated. "But I guess I don't get it. He's quite a bit older than you and he doesn't seem to be as into you as he could be. I'm explaining myself badly." Explaining himself badly or not, Adrik hung on every word. He needed someone to be honest with him. How did they look from an outsider's point of view? Legend tried again. "It's just that I didn't know there was anything between you two at all until you kissed him this morning. I've been trying to get your attention for a while, and I think you're amazing. If you were with me, everyone would know it. Why doesn't everyone know you're with him?"

Because Adrik was a mess, and that seemed the obvious answer. That was the answer Adrik should have been able to open his mouth and say. Instead, he wondered, was he with Leo? Or did Leo feel too sorry for him to push him away? When Adrik told Leo he loved him, did Leo say it back out of pity? Leo was worldlier than Adrik. Surely he had understood Legend wanted to be more than friends with Adrik, but he had left Adrik with Legend anyhow. Maybe he had hoped Adrik would move on. Damn.

Crippling pain sliced through Adrik. In his distress, he didn't know how to lie. "He saved me. I was brought to the US from Russia as a small child and sold to the highest-bidding pervert. After nearly twelve years of living a nightmare, Leo showed up and saved me. He's my hero." Adrik was Leo's mess. If Adrik loved him, he needed to be honest with himself, and be prepared to let Leo go.

Legend blinked several times. "Damn. I didn't see that one coming."

A humorless smile pulled at the corners of Adrik's mouth. "I guess going on dates for money doesn't seem so bad now, huh? You're so much better off without me. I had a lot of fun today. Thank you for letting me feel young. I'm sorry that I suck."

"You have no idea how much I wish..." Legend's wicked expression had a hot blush exploding across Adrik's face. He didn't know what to say. Legend was so much naughtier than Adrik knew how to be. Thankfully, Legend didn't force him to come up with a retort. He turned serious. "I don't for one second believe my life would be better without you in it. You're the first person I've spent time with in a long time who doesn't treat me like a whore. Can I still be your friend with high hopes that you'll fall madly in love with me one day?"

The backs of Adrik's eyes burned. He had been right earlier. That hint of unhappiness he had seen behind Legend's eyes was real. Adrik hated that Legend was anything other than the brightest star in the sky. "I would like that." Even Adrik heard the way his voice caught.

"All right, you sap. Give me a hug and I'll let you go inside."

Adrik willingly walked into Legend's arms. His heart squeezed in his chest. He cared about Legend. Adrik hated that he hurt him. He carried that sadness in the house with him after watching Legend walk away. Adrik toed off his shoes and tried to move quietly, hoping not to wake up Leo. He had a lot to think about. It was possible they needed to have an honest conversation. Adrik needed to accept that they weren't as close as Adrik built in his mind. Leo deserved to have someone whole. Adrik needed to sit down and figure out his life. Maybe he should stop trying to get his high school degree online and work full time for Zander. Then he could afford to live on his own. Maybe he wasn't that strong, but what choice did he have? Leo didn't want him for real.

Adrik understood that a little more with every passing moment.

"I was worried about you."

Adrik jumped and clutched his chest before doubling over and sucking air.

"I didn't mean to scare you," Leo said. His voice didn't change at all. Both statements sounded like he was talking about the weather, as if he hadn't just shaved ten years off Adrik's life.

While still sucking air, Adrik straightened. Leo sat in the dark, shirtless. With his feet on the coffee table and a bottle of Jack perched on his knee, he watched Adrik in a detached way. "I didn't see you sitting there."

"Yeah, I've been sitting here for a while, thinking."

Adrik crossed the room and pried the bottle from Leo's fingers. "And tying one on, apparently."

Leo looked damnably sober for someone who smelled like a distillery. "That too. Did you have fun?"

"I did. Thank you," Adrik said, setting the bottle on the table. "I ate way too much junk food and discovered I don't like heights. In fact, I discovered quite a few new things today."

"Was one of those things that you enjoyed that kiss outside?"

"What if it was?" Adrik shot back just as fast. He had planned to wait until Leo was sober and he had time to decide what to do before talking to Leo about them. It seemed Leo had other plans.

Leo leaned his head back and stared at Adrik in silence. "I shouldn't have asked that."

Part of Adrik wanted to take up the fight Leo was obviously fishing for, but the rest of Adrik wanted to forget his plan to set Leo free. He wasn't sure if he was brave enough to lose Leo. Pushing his plans aside, Adrik went with his gut. He threw one leg over Leo and straddled his lap. Leo's hands moved up Adrik's back, beneath his shirt.

"You came home confident."

Adrik started to push away. Leo didn't want this. Leo tightened his hold, refusing to let Adrik get away. He pulled Adrik closer and opened his mouth over Adrik's collarbone. Adrik's eyes fell closed. He sucked in a breath as his body immediately stirred at Leo's touch. His head fell back, giving Leo better access to his throat. Adrik's breathing turned ragged. Leo was hard beneath him. Adrik felt powerful—like he could do anything, because Leo's erection was for him. For the first time, Adrik truly wanted to strip away their clothes. He craved the sensation of Leo's bare skin against his. Adrik felt this way a lot in private. In fantasies. This was the first time he actually felt courageous enough to pull it off. The urge to watch as their cocks brushed was crippling him. He needed Leo.

Leo kissed a path from Adrik's collarbone up his neck until he reached Adrik's jaw. "You kissed him," Leo growled, sounding angry.

"Tell me not to do it again." Adrik surprised even himself with the demand. Once it was out there, he couldn't stop. "Tell me all my kisses belong to you. That I belong to you."

Leo slowly leaned away. He looked panicked. "I can't do that."

Leo should have punched him in the gut. It would have hurt less. It was exactly as he feared. Leo didn't want him. Not really. This was a physical response and even that wasn't strong enough to make Leo want him exclusively. Legend was right. They weren't a couple. The shaking struck from nowhere. He ground his teeth against it. Leo didn't want him. This was pity. Leo was scared to hurt him while silently wishing Adrik would find someone new.

Adrik climbed from Leo's lap. Leo didn't try to stop him. "I'm sorry." Those were the only words

Adrik could form through the pain. He kept his gaze averted as he headed for his room. Adrik had forced Leo to endure his tears too many times already. Leo had earned the right to be free of them. Adrik would do the adult thing. He would pack up his issues and move on. It was way past the time he should have given Leo his freedom. Adrik was too fucked up for anyone to truly love. He would go away.

FOUR

LEO TRAILED from one room to the next. His shock wouldn't let his brain function. There were pieces of Adrik everywhere. He had become too entrenched in Leo's life to take everything in one trip, but enough of Adrik's existence was missing to punch a hole in Leo's chest. He had consumed way too much alcohol to hear Adrik leave. When Leo had finally passed out after Adrik fled to his bedroom, he had done it right. Leo had not opened his eyes again until the sun blasted him with fury, splitting his head. Then, there it had been. The note that carried Adrik from his life.

After confirming Adrik was indeed gone, Leo moved back to the couch. His gaze dropped to the note he still clutched to his chest, trying to patch the hole left there from Adrik ripping out his heart. He had polished off enough Jack that he had lost control of his tongue, but his memory worked just fine. Legend had kissed Adrik. Adrik let it happen. The rage had been real. But Adrik had come inside to him. He had straddled Leo's lap in a show of beautiful bravery. Adrik had taunted Leo with his dreams, demanding Leo say all the things he couldn't. Leo couldn't become the man who had kept Adrik against his will. He needed to be the one person whose love was free.

Adrik's messy handwriting scrawled across the paper. He didn't write often, choosing instead to use his computer to print off notes, because his handwriting was still years below his age. For Leo, Adrik had written this final note by hand. Leo's heart couldn't take it. He needed every piece of Adrik. His gaze slid across the words, taking them in again, and searching for answers.

Leo,

I wish I was strong enough to do this in person. When I think back on all our time together, I can't remember a time when I haven't been in love with you. It wasn't fair for you to be saddled with my love. You saved me. How am I supposed to thank you for that? Do you have any idea how special you are in my eyes? You're everything. It guts me to think you spent two and half years stuck with me. No one deserves that. So I've already called Legend. He'll be here in a few minutes. This is me, setting you free. Promise me you'll be happy. Swear you won't waste another day worrying over my health and mental state. Don't think about if I can handle life or if I'll finally end up institutionalized. All of that is on me now. I need to know you're happy. You'll never be complete with me. I'm sorry that I stole so much time from you. It won't happen again. Thank you for being everything to me when I had nothing. I will never forget you.

Love, Adrik

He was completely unprepared for the pain. Leo had to talk to him. Adrik needed to explain this letter. Unfortunately, when Leo found himself calling Adrik's cell phone, he was unprepared for the words that left his lips as Adrik answered.

"You had Legend come get you in the middle of the night."

A long, heavy pause stretched on. Finally, Adrik cleared his throat. "I didn't feel comfortable calling anyone else."

Leo took a slow breath. His head pounded. Everything hurt. Anger he didn't want grew. "I was right here. You didn't have to go to him."

"Yes, I did." Adrik answered way too fast for Leo's sanity. "I've spent two and a half years taking from you."

Leo hung up. He couldn't. Seriously. Leo couldn't listen to Adrik choose someone else. He had honestly believed he could accept Adrik choosing Legend. Fuck that guy. He didn't love Adrik. Leo was the one who worried day and night. He was the one who had stayed up nights through the nightmares and the anger. Leo had been to counseling and doctor appointments. Surgeries and testing. He had been right there, showing his love every damn day. Legend didn't get to take Adrik to the goddamn carnival one day and sweep Adrik away. Except that was exactly what he had done, and Leo didn't know if he could live with that.

WORKING WITH ZANDER WAS NORMALLY peaceful. Adrik wasn't old enough to go inside the casino. That fact gave him the perfect excuse to stick to the hotel and office areas where it was quiet. Normally, he stuck close to either Zander or one of Zander's bodyguards. Adrik liked the silence of the place, but he didn't like being unaccompanied.

Today, he had borrowed Justice's office just so he could be alone. He didn't want anyone looking at him since Leo hung up on him. Adrik also didn't want to risk running into Leo, if he had to stop by for work. While Leo didn't swing by during Adrik's shifts every day, Adrik was not taking any chances.

It ended up being Yaro who found him sitting on the floor behind Justice's desk, watching security footage on his laptop and crying like an idiot.

"Oh, *Kishka*, what is all this?"

Even through his tears, Adrik couldn't help but smile over getting called kitten. He swiped at his face and paused the video. "Don't worry over me. I'm just having a day."

Yaro's gaze moved from Adrik to his bags, which were still sitting in the corner, and back to Adrik. "Did you sleep here?"

It wasn't like he could lie. It was one thing to let Legend think he planned to stay at the hotel, and another to lie to Yaro. The man was like family. Adrik swallowed and nodded. "Justice said I could use his office whenever I need. He didn't mean like this, but I didn't have anywhere else to go."

Yaro joined him on the floor. His odd-colored eyes were full of concern. "What happened to staying at Leo's?"

Adrik shook his head. More tears fell. It was like someone had turned the spigot on the moment he was alone and now the tears wouldn't stop falling. "I can't stay there anymore."

"You want Yaro to break his spindly legs? He means nothing to me."

A watery laugh escaped Adrik. "No. It's not his fault. He doesn't love me like I love him." The confession came without his permission, but once it was out there, he couldn't stop. "I don't want to keep his life on hold anymore because I'm broken and who the hell wants this?" Adrik motioned toward himself with all the disgust he felt in his heart.

"You will stay with Yaro. We will do all the fun stuff. Eat junk food. Ooooh, get facial. That is amazing. People have it so easy here."

Despite the situation, Adrik couldn't help but smile at this gigantic man getting excited over a facial. "I've never had one of those, but I couldn't intrude on your home." Because Yaro lived with Zander, and Adrik could not be any farther in Zander's debt.

"No intrusion. The place is so big, no one would even notice you were there. You can't stay here. What will you eat?"

Adrik shrugged. "I've gone hungry before."

"Psssh," Yaro said, blowing out a breath. "You may be a tiny *kishka*, but Yaro will not let you starve." He looked around. "Or sleep on the floor. You are not a prisoner anymore. Zander would be very upset to know you are no longer at Leo's. He might have Pytor hop over there and break his kneecaps no matter your opinion. That was very reckless of him to let you go, knowing you have no place to stay. I'm very upset about this. You better agree to stay with us, or I'll send my man over there." Yaro's nostrils flared and Adrik scrambled to fix it.

"Don't send Pytor. I'll stay with you, but seriously, it's not Leo's fault."

"Oh, good. Let's go," Yaro said, popping to his feet like a much younger and smaller man. He scooped up Adrik's bags before he could argue. Adrik watched it happen with a sense of unreality. He had a bad feeling his life had just been commandeered. Not that it mattered. Adrik wasn't doing such a good job of steering this ship anyhow. Yaro couldn't do worse.

MAYBE ADRIK WAS DONE WITH LEO, BUT LEO wasn't finished with Adrik. He was Leo's responsibility. Adrik wouldn't take care of himself if Leo didn't make him. It seemed at least that much hadn't changed, since they were on day three of the pharmacy reminding him Adrik hadn't picked up his prescriptions. Leo couldn't let that go on, no matter how much it hurt seeing Adrik with someone else. His knuckles skimmed Legend's front door. The guy had a nice place. It seemed selling his time and company paid well. He wondered if Adrik knew what Legend did to pay for this place. Most likely not. Selling his body wasn't something that would sit well with someone like Adrik.

The door swung open. Legend stood—shirtless and reminding Leo of their difference in age. Leo would never look that good again. Leo tried looking in every direction but Legend's. He couldn't look directly at the man who had won Adrik. "I have Adrik's meds. He does okay working part time at the casino, but he's on a lot expensive prescriptions. That's why I have him listed as my domestic partner on my insurance at work. Even with my insurance, these two are pricey, so I picked them up." Even though Leo knew he was rambling, he couldn't help it. "Here," he said, holding out the bag so the words would stop coming.

Legend didn't take it. "That's cool of you to help

out Adrik, but I don't know why you're giving them to me."

At Legend's words, Leo found himself finally looking directly at him. "Because he's staying here, right?"

"Um, no." Legend sounded like he didn't know if he should lie or not. It was obvious his loyalty was firmly in Adrik's camp.

Leo's brow furrowed. "It's okay. I'm not mad." That might not be strictly true, but still. Adrik's health came first.

Legend leaned into the door frame and crossed his arms over his chest. "I don't know why you would be angry. He's not staying here. A, Adrik doesn't want me. B, he's in love with you, and C, he's already told me he doesn't want me, because he's in love with you. You really have no right to be mad."

It wasn't that Leo tried to be an obtuse ass, but he was confused. "Sorry, I thought Adrik said he was staying here, but now I'm not sure if that's what he said or..." if that was what Leo had assumed he meant. Fuck. Where was Adrik?

Legend sighed and straightened away from the door frame. "He's staying at some really huge-ass house on the beach with friends. Let me see." He pulled his phone from his back pocket and scrolled through his texts. "I have the address in here somewhere. It's..."

"400 Ocean Port," Leo said at the same time as Legend said, "400 Ocean Port. Yeah," Legend confirmed with a laugh, obviously not hearing the defeat in Leo's tone. "He said some guys from work said he could crash with them for as long as he wanted. I went to see him the other night. They had some hellacious security. Thought I might get strip searched. Not that I'm opposed," he added with a wink.

Damn. Leo hadn't expected to have to go to Zander's today. In fact, if he had taken Adrik in, Zander probably knew all Leo's sins and might not let him see Adrik at all. Just when Leo thought things couldn't possibly get worse, life threw him another curveball. Jesus, he hated everything. "Thanks, man. I guess I'll head that way."

Legend reached out, stopping Leo before he could get away. His expression turned serious. He looked older and more exhausted than Leo had ever noticed before. "I know you're a good guy, so you'll listen and hear what I'm about to say. If you don't want to be with Adrik, you should find another way to get his meds to him other than taking them yourself. It's bad. I don't think you realize how much you mean to him. This separation or whatever you two have going on." Legend shook his head. "It's ugly. You're not doing him any favors by going over there."

He knew Legend's words came from a good place, but Leo had been taking care of Adrik longer. There was nothing Adrik could throw his way that would make Leo stop loving him. "I've got him." Whether Legend believed it was true or not, mattered not at all. Adrik was his. Leo would take care of him.

UNHAPPINESS WEIGHED SO MUCH. ADRIK DIDN'T understand why he wasn't as muscular as Zander's MMA champion husband. He had been carrying around misery his entire life. It wasn't fair for him to be scrawny and depressed. Some people had it all. Adrik had nothing. Even the cavernous room with an indoor waterfall that he currently enjoyed wasn't his. He was a visitor. Another pity home. Adrik had fallen down such a deep pit of depression, he had stopped doing everything. Zander wouldn't let him work full time. Instead, he had opened an account for Adrik and dumped a massive load of money into it. No one seemed to notice or care he didn't want it. Adrik stopped attending his online classes. No one gave a fuck he didn't understand most forms of math. He didn't eat. Adrik wasn't completely sure when he had something to drink last. He didn't care. The only good thing about life was that everyone basically left him in peace. Legend had come to visit. Pytor checked to make sure he was still breathing a couple of times a day. Otherwise, Adrik was free to wallow and think. He knew he should rub two brain cells together and plan his future. The desire wasn't there.

The sound of the waterfall drowned out everything but the black emotions that owned him. Adrik's eyes burned, reminding him to blink. It was odd how many things he simply forgot to do. He rarely moved at all. Adrik might have forgotten to breathe if it wasn't automatic.

A white pharmacy style bag appeared in front of his face. Adrik followed the line of the man's arm. His gaze landed on his heart. Pain exploded through Adrik. He looked away.

Leo set the bag on Adrik's lap and filled the chair beside him.

"How much do I owe you?" Even Adrik heard the way his voice sounded dead and like he hadn't had a drop of water in days.

"An explanation."

Adrik felt nothing but the crippling pain. "I left you a note. If that wasn't enough for you, you shouldn't have hung up on me."

"You kissed Legend and then had him come pick you up in the middle of the night. I was hungover, pissed about all of that, and you're right. I shouldn't have hung up on you."

Adrik didn't understand Leo at all. He confused Adrik like no one else. "Technically, Legend kissed me, and I pushed him away. Being hungover was your own damn fault, and I asked you to tell me we're exclusive and you said no. You don't want me. You don't want anyone else to have me. I know I'm pathetic, but do you really expect me to be alone for the rest of my life because I'm damaged? That's shitty." There should have been fire in Adrik's words. He felt the anger and hurt, but he just sounded tired. Maybe he had already given up on this life.

"I want you."

Adrik tried and failed at suppressing a snort. "Stop pitying me. I won't die if you admit you don't love me the way I love you. It's okay. I get that I'm a mess and that's not attractive at all. Just stop playing the martyr. You're free."

"I don't want to be free." Leo never once stopped

sounding calm. It hurt. Leo's peace was everything Adrik needed, and it killed Adrik because he couldn't have him. Before Adrik could say as much, Leo continued. "Sometimes, I don't know the right thing to do. I'm learning as I go with you. But, I guess, I thought you knew we were exclusive. Then I saw you with Legend at the gym. You were laughing and having fun. I thought, maybe you needed that in your life." Adrik met the amber stare he loved and didn't look away. He needed to see Leo's sincerity. Leo didn't stop. "If you want me to demand that you keep all your kisses for me, I don't know that I can do that. Not because they're not mine. We both know they are, but because I don't own you. If you choose someone else, then you do. It'll absolutely break me, but I won't stop you. You're free to make every decision that any other human is allowed to make. I don't want to be possessive, even though I am. To me, you're mine. I don't want to be jealous, but I am. Part of me still wants to break Legend's legs. But you're free to leave me, if that's what you want."

Adrik's eyes stung, but he was all cried out. His throat burned. He was scared to believe. Adrik didn't know if he could keep losing Leo over and over again. "I thought." Adrik stopped to clear his throat when his voice cracked. He tried again. "I thought you were scared to admit that you wanted out, and I didn't want to hold you hostage with my love anymore. You deserve so much more than me." Adrik swallowed. Tears he didn't think he still had threatened to spill. "You saved me, and I feel like I'm killing you."

A sad smile touched Leo's lips. "You are right now, because you're here, and you belong with me. I want to kiss you and tell you I love you, but you took away that right. Maybe I'm just too serious for you to keep."

He loved Leo. There would never be anyone else. Adrik dug deep and pulled out the strength for one more try. "Could I take you to dinner tonight? Obviously, I can't drive," Adrik added with a nervous chuckle. "But I can pay and call a cab."

"Or I could pick you up."

Adrik bit his bottom lip, trying not to smile. "Or you could pick me up." Adrik knew he could go home. Leo would pack him up and take him back home. All Adrik had to do was ask. The thing was, he didn't want that. He didn't want to sweep this under the rug and go back to who they had been. Leo deserved to go on a real date. He deserved a normal relationship with a regular guy. Adrik would be that person, even if it terrified him.

"Would it be okay if I kissed you?" Leo's voice cracked on the question and Adrik knew this wasn't pity. Leo loved Adrik every bit as much as Adrik loved Leo.

"Yes."

Leo pulled his chair close. Adrik's eyes fell closed as their lips met. He licked Leo's bottom lip, going for more. Leo's lips parted and Adrik delved inside, stroking Leo's tongue with his. He moved tentatively at first. Then Leo shifted closer. Adrik's head fell back beneath his attack. It was perfect. There was no fear. He was with his hero. Nothing bad could happen to him in Leo's arms.

Leo's lips moved to the corner of Adrik's mouth. "So," he said against Adrik's skin and between kisses. "Why are you hanging out by the parkour course?"

Adrik chuckled. "I don't know what that is. I just found a peaceful spot and sat."

Leo pulled away and touched his forehead to Adrik's. He was even more beautiful up close. "Ask Pytor and Yaro to give you a demonstration."

Adrik nodded, squishing their foreheads together. "See you when you get off work?"

Leo pressed another lingering kiss to the corner of Adrik's mouth. "I'll be here."

As Adrik accepted one more kiss, he did

something he never did. He prayed. Even though there was a good ninety-eight percent of Adrik that didn't believe in God, that other two percent held out hope. Adrik needed his help. If there was a God, he needed the man to make him whole, because Adrik couldn't fail Leo anymore. This was the last chance he would give himself. Adrik had to be strong.

FIVE

CONSIDERING Leo and Adrik had spent almost every day together for the last two and a half years, Leo shouldn't be nervous. He thought he might be sick. Despite talking through things and recognizing their faults, Adrik had not come home. Instead, he had asked Leo on a date. It felt like a test. Leo had never been good at those. He was good at being reliable and steady. That was how he made himself invaluable at all things. That wouldn't be enough to get Adrik back home.

He still couldn't believe Adrik thought his love was only out of pity. Leo had been so busy trying to go slow, he had forgotten to be open. He hadn't wanted to scare Adrik with his desire, but god knew he wanted Adrik. Every aspect of him. Forever. Leo had already begun working on a new plan. It would take a couple of days and some help from his friends. Right now, he needed to focus on getting through tonight.

Going back to Zander's was like walking through a firing squad to get to Adrik. The second time was no easier than the first. Yaro still wasn't speaking to him. Even though Yaro was a mountain of a man, he was a gentle giant. He seemed genuinely injured on Adrik's behalf. Yaro wouldn't even look his way. Leo decided to face one battle at a time. Two battles turned into three when he found Adrik still hanging out at the indoor exercise course. This time, he wasn't alone. In shorts and a t-shirt, Adrik was being helped to scale the waterfall climbing wall by Pytor and Legend. Pytor looked like a fucking house perched on the wall, yelling directions to Adrik, who wasn't doing bad, to Leo's surprise. Legend was beneath him, poised to catch Adrik if he fell. Leo wanted to put his fist through Legend's too pretty face, but he didn't want to distract the guy in case he really did need to catch Adrik.

"That's enough for tonight, little one," Pytor yelled. "Your date is waiting."

Adrik glanced over his shoulder and smiled at the sight of Leo waiting. "Hi."

Leo's heart rose into his throat. He was scared shitless for Adrik's safety. "Hey, baby."

"Let go, sweets. The pretty boy will catch you."

To Leo's surprise, Adrik immediately dropped and Legend easily snagged him from the air. Adrik wore a huge smile as he rushed to Leo's side. "Did you see me? I got that high all by myself."

"You were amazing, gorgeous." Leo's heart still pounded, but Adrik looked so happy.

"Come on," Adrik said, taking his hand and dragging him down the hall. He spoke over his shoulder along the way. "I lost track of time. If you don't mind hanging out for a bit, I'll jump in the shower."

Leo would wait forever for a minute of Adrik's time. "Do whatever you need. I'm not going anywhere."

Adrik led him inside a huge bedroom. The place was as big as Leo's entire house. Leo sat on the edge of the king-sized bed and watched Adrik dig through the dresser for clothes. He had unpacked his bags— like he planned to stay. As hard as Leo tried clinging to hope, he wasn't sure he was winning.

Adrik moved to Leo's side and dumped his clothes on the bed before tugging his shirt up and over his head. Before he could get away, Leo snagged his waist and hauled him to stand between his knees. Adrik didn't look nervous. He was gaining confidence beneath the exercises everyone kept convincing him to try.

"You look happy here."

Adrik's face softened. His hands ran up Leo's arms until he linked his fingers behind Leo's neck. He shuffled closer. "I look happy because you're here. I was able to let go and have fun because I knew you were on your way."

"It surprised me to see Legend here." Damn. He didn't like himself tonight.

Adrik's smile grew. "Pytor and Yaro invited him to come play after I did as you suggested and asked them for a demonstration. You sound so jealous right now. That's never happened before." Adrik chuckled and lowered his voice, as if someone might hear and judge him. "Is it wrong that I like it a little?"

Leo found himself massaging Adrik's hips and pulling him closer. "Damn, you're beautiful. I'm jealous a lot, but I keep it to myself. You're looking at me like we might not make it to dinner."

Adrik leaned closer. "I promised to feed you and I will. You smell good." He dipped his head and buried his nose against Leo's neck. Chill bumps rose on Leo's skin. His cock stirred. Adrik kissed his neck.

"You're also making me feel underdressed. I should get in the shower." He didn't move away.

"Adrik." Even Leo heard the longing in his voice. He was so in love with Adrik and they had been apart, breaking Leo's heart. "Kiss me first."

Adrik's lips brushed his neck. Leo's breath caught in his throat. Adrik moved slow, kissing a path to Leo's mouth. By the time their tongues brushed, Leo was so hard, he ached. Adrik felt good in his arms. Leo fought the urge to massage every place he could reach. Their kiss turned heated. Leo's hands found Adrik's ass. He was half a second from hauling Adrik into bed. The familiar sound of the alarm on Adrik's phone blared through the room.

"Dang," Adrik said, pulling away. "Medicine time." His cheeks were flushed, and he looked turned on. He was beautiful. Adrik cast a look around. "Crap. I forgot my drink."

Leo urged Adrik back, making room to stand. "Go get in the shower. I'll go back and get it."

Adrik nodded, looking disappointed. "Okay. Thanks. It's a blue cup. You know, one of those stainless-steel things with a straw. I left it on the floor near the rocky side of their ninja course thing."

Leo brushed his lips across Adrik's one last time. "On it." He headed for the door, trying to breathe through his nose. The last thing Leo wanted was to run into anyone with a hard-on. Luckily, his body cooled enough to spare him embarrassment by the time he made it back to Zander's indoor warrior course. Yaro, Pytor, and Legend were standing around shirtless and barefoot, obviously getting ready to race. No one looked his way as he went on the hunt for Adrik's cup.

"How long have you two been together?"

Leo didn't want to listen, but it was impossible not to hear. Plus, he was kind of curious to hear the answer to Legend's question.

Yaro was the one to respond. "This one stole a kiss from me when we were six." Yaro laughed as he spoke. "I told my momma I would marry him someday. She made me swear not to tell anyone else. It is dangerous to prefer men where we are from. When our first boss, Gio, had to make a trip to the Netherlands in two thousand and two, we sneaked away and married in secret. But we have always been together."

That was sweet. Leo couldn't help but smile at the thought.

"You were adorable, even at six," Pytor said, making Leo suppress a chuckle at the image of either one of these giants being adorable.

"Do you see someone?" Yaro asked, sounding genuinely interested in hearing Legend's answer.

Leo took his time. He was oddly fascinated by the conversation. Over the last few years, he had spent a lot of time around Pytor and Yaro. This was the most he had heard the men speak to anyone except each other. Plus, he wanted to hear Legend's answer to Pytor's question. If he had kissed Adrik while dating someone else, they were about to throw down. It didn't matter Adrik belonged to Leo. No one treated him like that.

"Nah. I work as an escort. That's a huge thing to overlook. No one wants to date me."

Pytor and Yaro shared an evil-sounding chuckle. "We would pay good money to have you keep us company."

"I'm keeping you company now for free."

Welp. Leo had stayed too long. He snatched up Adrik's cup and got out of dodge before he learned too much. Leo made it back to Adrik's room in no time in his rush to get away. As he came through the door, Leo expected Adrik to be in the shower. Instead, he still stood where Leo had left him. Except now he was nude, hard, and obviously waiting for Leo's return. His glasses were missing— like he didn't truly want to see Leo's reaction.

Adrik blushed but didn't look away. "I was starting to think you weren't coming back."

Leo crossed the room, trying not to pounce. Adrik was perfect in his eyes. "I had to hunt a bit to find your cup." He set it on the bedside table before moving to stand over Adrik. "I thought you'd be in the shower."

Adrik shook his head. "Not yet. I still promise to feed you, but I hoped you might take me to bed first." Adrik's blush deepened. He was so adorable.

Leo didn't want to make Adrik's embarrassment worse, but he needed to know how far Adrik wanted him to go. "I would love that. But first, I need you to tell me where to draw the line." Adrik looked uncomfortable—like his courage slipped. Leo didn't want that. "You can tell me as we go," Leo said, setting Adrik free. He dipped his head and captured Adrik's lips. Leo needed Adrik's bravery back. As their tongues stroked, Leo lifted Adrik's feet from the floor and eased him down on the bed. He pulled away only long enough to toss away his shirt. When he reclaimed Adrik's mouth, Adrik worked on Leo's belt and button. His breath left him as Adrik's fingers closed around his erection. Leo already knew it wouldn't take much to make him blow. His body recognized its owner.

"Tell me what you want to try," Leo begged between kisses. He wanted everything, and he was scared to fuck this up.

Adrik kissed Leo's neck and openly caressed Leo's cock. When he answered, Leo swore he could hear the horror in Adrik's voice, but he didn't back down. "Maybe you could sort of flip around so I can lick this while you do the same."

Jesus. Leo nearly came right then. Adrik was the sexiest version of innocence he had ever seen. He wanted that. "I love this plan." He rolled and stripped off his pants before Adrik could change his mind. Leo made a point of not meeting Adrik's stare as he flipped around. He already knew how Adrik felt about being watched. Instead, he went straight for the prize and swallowed Adrik's cock. Adrik gasped. Leo concentrated on his job, trying not to beg for Adrik's touch. It came hesitantly at first. His fingers lightly encircled Leo's erection. Leo held his breath. The softest of licks stroked his crown. Leo's stomach muscles jumped. Adrik's every move was crippling pleasure, because it was Adrik. If Adrik needed practice or lacked any skill, Leo didn't notice. He was way too aroused to consider anything but how fucked his mind was at the moment. With Adrik sucking just the tip of Leo's dick like a lollipop, Leo already knew he wouldn't last. He couldn't let Adrik be disappointed.

Leo put his heart into pleasuring Adrik. He took Adrik down his throat over and over, letting the saliva flow. Leo used his hands, pumping and wetting his fingers before toying with Adrik's balls and hole. Adrik moved against Leo's mouth without shame. His whimpers around Leo's cock were driving Leo insane. He pumped out pre-cum at nearly the rate of an orgasm. Leo had never been more turned on in his life. He curled one finger inside Adrik's ass, massaging his prostate. Adrik's entire body stiffened. A cry filled the air. Cum flooded Leo's mouth. Adrik went wild on Leo's dick. Leo fought for air as he tried swallowing Adrik's load with ecstasy dancing on his cock. Adrik held him in a tight grip while sucking hard on his crown. Leo saw stars as an orgasm tore through him. He expected Adrik to pull away. Adrik didn't stop. He sucked, stealing Leo's soul along with every ounce of cum in Leo's body. Leo was a shaking, gasping mess beneath Adrik's ministrations. While he melted into a useless puddle, Adrik shifted and kissed a path up Leo's body. He stopped at Leo's chin, as if scared Leo wouldn't kiss him after having Leo's dick in his mouth. Fuck that. Leo hauled him upward and captured Adrik's mouth. He licked and sucked, making it clear he loved the taste of cum on Adrik's tongue. Adrik kissed him back every bit as fiercely. This was love. He didn't want Adrik to ever forget again.

"Let's stay in bed," Leo pled. "We can order a pizza and just stay right here."

"My arms and legs are protesting that climb, so that's probably the smart thing to do." The laughter in Adrik's voice made even Leo's heart smile.

"I love you so much." Leo couldn't hold back the words. He was so over the top in love with Adrik. Leo didn't know how to play it cool.

"I love you too, baby," Adrik said, stealing more kisses. "I'm trying to be whole for you."

Adrik's claim broke Leo's heart. "Oh, baby." He pushed Adrik's dark hair away from his face and held his face between his hands, leaving Adrik no choice but to look at him. He needed Adrik to see and hear the truth. "You are perfect to me. Okay? I don't know how to prove it to you, but I have never had a single complaint about our relationship. I'm happy being with you. Just as you are."

A small smile crossed Adrik's lips. "I know, but I need to be whole for you for my sake. Because I can't keep doing crazy crap, trying to destroy us for whatever sneaks into my brain next. So I need you to know I'm trying."

"I've always known that." Leo wished Adrik saw himself the way Leo did. "You're the bravest and strongest person I've ever met. A lot of people believe in you, but I believe in you more than anyone. I know you won't break. It's me who can't handle losing you." Adrik had the lightest eyes Leo had ever seen. They were so beautiful and filled with love. Leo couldn't take it. "Please come back home to me." His voice cracked on the plea. Leo couldn't go back to his empty house and cracked heart. Nothing was right without Adrik. "I'll understand if you can't, but I'm dying without you."

A sweet smile touched Adrik's lips. "We're stupid. Did you know that?"

"Okay." Leo didn't try to hide his confusion.

Adrik shook his head and laughed. "We ended up here because we don't talk to each other, and I'm still here because I didn't know if you wanted me to come home, so I was determined to win you. Do you think we'll ever learn to just say what we want?"

A snort escaped Leo. He couldn't stop the sound. Adrik was right. They were stupid. Leo toyed with Adrik's hair. "Well, I mean, this is a nice room. I suppose one night might feel like a mini vacation and we could go home in the morning."

"And we haven't ordered our pizza yet," Adrik said, adding his two cents. "It seems to me like waiting until tomorrow is best."

Leo couldn't stop smiling. He knew he had met his other half. Leo had known for a long time. Now all he had to do was convince Adrik to keep him forever, and he already had a plan brewing for that. Things were definitely looking up.

SIX

A LIGHT SUCTION on his cock pulled Leo from a deep sleep. He gasped. His fingers found Adrik's hair. A moan dragged from his throat. Adrik treated him like this was his favorite thing to do and waking up this way was heaven.

"I'm feeling our age difference. You have so much more energy than I do. I don't want to move. Goddamn. That feels good." It was like each sexual encounter bolstered Adrik's confidence and wiped away his fear. Leo had no complaints about Adrik using him to heal.

Adrik massaged as he sucked, rolling Leo's eyes back in his head. He stroked the spot between Leo's balls and asshole. His lips skimmed Leo's cock.

"Tell me how to do what you did to me."

Leo sucked air. He had never been more aroused. It took a moment for Leo to grasp what Adrik meant. Adrik circled Leo's hole with his fingertip, leaving no doubt what he meant. "Um." He tried gathering his scattered thoughts. "You'll have to feel for the right spot." Adrik's finger pushed its way in. Leo scratched at the sheets. His mind was a mess. "If you curl your finger a bit and push up." Adrik did as told. Leo nearly came as Adrik hit the right spot. A deep moan vibrated from his chest.

"I feel it," Adrik said, sounding excited.

Leo fought a smile. It died on a gasp as Adrik put his new knowledge to use. Then Adrik lips locked around Leo's crown. He sucked. Leo blew. There was barely any warning. He was locked inside the pleasure overtaking his body. Leo couldn't do anything but gasp for air while Adrik stroked him. Adrik kissed his stomach, moving higher. "Will you come take a shower with me?"

Leo wasn't sure his legs worked anymore, but he wasn't saying no. This was the greatest love of his life. Leo still needed to make him fly. "Yeah. I'm on it." Even with his brave words out there, it took Leo a minute to find the strength. Only the sight of Adrik's erection got Leo moving. He couldn't let Adrik suffer unfulfilled.

The shower was a work of art. The ceiling was a giant rain shower while jets shot out in several directions. He let Adrik set the water temperature, which was a little hot for Leo's tastes, but he knew he would live. Leo held Adrik while water hit them from every angle. The sensation of Adrik's bare skin against Leo's nude body was nirvana. Leo washed Adrik and teased him, stroking everywhere but where Adrik needed him. By the time Leo held Adrik with his back against Leo's chest and encircled Adrik's cock, his own dick was hard enough to bend steel again. Not that Leo intended to do anything about it. He simply enjoyed the way Adrik moved restlessly against him. His slick and soapy ass wiggled against Leo's cock, making his mind fuzzy.

Leo took his time, slowly pumping Adrik's erection. His lips teased Adrik's neck. There was so much love filling Leo's chest, he wondered if he would burst. He had always loved Adrik. Adding this part was only icing. If Leo had the chance to do nothing except be right here with Adrik, Leo would accept it in a heartbeat. Despite their age differences, Leo wanted to spend the rest of his life with Adrik. They were meant to be.

Adrik reached over his head and gripped the back of Leo's neck, holding him in place to kiss his throat. He moved against Leo's hand, openly taking his pleasure. "I love you, Leo. Please, Leo."

Leo quickened his pace at the plea. He needed his baby to soar. A whimper reverberated off the walls of the shower as jets of cum shot through the air. Leo worked to shake out every drop. Adrik was a gasping mess against Leo's chest. Only Leo's arm around his waist kept Adrik upright. There would likely be a hickey on Adrik's neck. He couldn't stop himself from gnawing on Adrik. His flavor was addicting. Leo couldn't say exactly when he had fallen so deep for Adrik. All he knew was he had looked over one day and Adrik was everything to him. He knew they needed to go home. They couldn't linger at Zander's forever. Still, Leo didn't rush. He had some vacation time built up. It seemed a good time to take it. He needed to do some things, because he couldn't ever let Adrik get away again. This relationship meant everything to him.

LEO KEPT TOSSING HOT GLANCES HIS WAY AS they dressed and Adrik could barely take it. He wanted to go back to bed. Adrik had never been able to stand anyone's touch, but Leo wasn't just anyone.

They had spent the entire night nude and touching. Leo had fallen asleep sticky and clinging to Adrik. It had been the best night of Adrik's life. He didn't want this time alone and sequestered to end. They needed to go back home. Adrik didn't hurry.

"We should hit the kitchen before I pack. I think you need some water and protein."

Leo's laughter kept Adrik from blushing as he made the suggestion. He loved making Leo smile. Leo circled the bed and pulled Adrik into his arms. He was so sexy. Adrik loved looking at Leo. His amber-colored eyes were unique and beautiful. Just like Leo's soul. "You're probably right," Leo said, leaning over to nuzzle Adrik's neck. "I need fortification to keep up with you." Adrik giggled as Leo blew against Adrik's neck, making noises. Leo stroked his ass before pulling away. "Also, Justice stopped by the other night. He had some questions for you about that list you gave them."

"Questions?" Adrik had no clue what anyone thought he might know that they didn't.

Leo nodded. "He asked if you'd noticed anything odd about it. I figured we'd swing by the casino and see what's going on, if that's okay with you?"

"Huh. Okay. I'll take a look at it again on the way over and see if I can figure out what he thinks is odd.

But first, food." He herded Leo toward the door. He was starving. Since he had left Leo's, Adrik had barely eaten a thing. Zander's fridge was always stocked with the best food.

Leo dragged his feet, being purposely obnoxious. "Hey, Adrik. You know what?"

Adrik pushed, trying to get him moving. Damn, Leo was solid as hell. "What?"

"I love you."

Adrik tried holding on to his patience. "I love you too."

Leo only managed two steps but somehow kept the entire doorway blocked. "You know what else?"

A growl rose in Adrik's throat. "What?"

"I love you more."

Adrik's eye twitched. "For fuck's sake."

Leo threw his head back and roared with laughter. "You said a bad word." He swiped at his eyes. "You're so cranky when you're hungry. It's adorable."

Even after taking a breath, Adrik barely suppressed the urge to stomp Leo's foot.

Leo tucked Adrik against his side. "All right, cranky butt. Let's get some food in you."

Adrik held on to his irritation all the way to the kitchen. The moment Leo popped a mini donut in his mouth, Adrik's temper slipped away. He felt a bit stupid for getting snippy. Adrik chewed, letting the sugar touch his soul while Leo poured him some orange juice.

Adrik swallowed. "By the way, you don't love me more."

Leo glanced his way and winked.

Adrik accepted the glass from Leo and leaned back against the counter. He loved watching Leo move around the kitchen. This wasn't the house's main kitchen. It was a smaller one that was meant for preparing light meals taken in the sunroom. Adrik hadn't seen any staff moving about the house, but there was always fruit and other healthy snacks sitting around. The kitchen was white and oak. It was cozy and perfect in Adrik's eyes. It was just the place for guests who wanted a small meal in peace.

Legend appeared in the doorway—shirtless and looking like hell. His blond hair was a mess and there were smudges beneath his eyes. He looked almost embarrassed to find them in the kitchen. He tried shuffling into the room—like he hoped they would pretend he wasn't there.

Adrik was feeling too happy this morning for that nonsense. "Good morning. You look like you had a full night."

Legend kept his face averted as he dug through the fridge and came out with a bottle of water. "Yeah. We got carried away and ended up staying up all night."

Adrik noticed Leo pointedly did not look Legend's way. He wondered how long Leo planned to stay mad at Legend over that kiss. Adrik decided to talk to both men and hope they would get over this. "What time do you have to be at work, Leo?"

Leo worked on making toast. "I'm not going in today. In fact, I think I'll take some of my built-up vacation time."

That sounded amazing to Adrik. Leo never took time off unless he was doing a different job for Zander. "Yay."

Leo flashed him a smile.

Adrik looked Legend's way. He was easing toward the door. "Hey, Legend. Do you think— sometime—we could make plans to meet up here and work some more on that obstacle course?"

"Um." Legend looked uncomfortable as hell. "I don't know if I should." He sounded nervous. "I mean. You're a natural and Pytor and Yaro are here."

"Oh." Adrik's heart sank. This wouldn't work. That one kiss had been too much, it seemed. Leo had forgiven Adrik, but he wouldn't get to keep Legend as a friend. He didn't understand social rules. Adrik hadn't grown up normal. He didn't grasp who could be friends with whom, and under what circumstances. It seemed he could be friends with Legend and not date Leo, or he could date Leo, but he couldn't still be Legend's friend. It was depressing.

"If you want, and it's okay with Leo, I'll still work with you on the self-defense stuff at the gym."

Leo barely spared them a glance. "Why would I care? Adrik can be friends with whoever he wants."

Adrik smiled. They were talking. That made Adrik happy. His happiness fled as quickly as it hit. They had been friends before Legend had tried being Adrik's friend too, but now they weren't anymore. Now they were tiptoeing around each other. He didn't like this. "Please stop." The words burst from him louder than he intended. Both men turned his way, looking more than a little shocked by his outburst.

Leo's furrowed brow showed his worry. "What's wrong?"

"Stop being angry because of me. I don't like it. I feel like my clothes are too tight and I can't breathe properly. Just stop." He couldn't look directly at anyone. He hated when things felt off kilter. Adrik needed his little world to run smoothly, or he felt like he choked on air. Sometimes, panic hit at the oddest times when the tiniest detail was out of alignment.

"Nobody's mad, sweetie," Legend said, setting his water aside and moving closer.

Leo nodded. "We're fine." He closed the distance between them and rubbed Adrik's arms. "You don't have to keep the peace, baby. Everything is okay. Take a breath."

Adrik did as he said, realizing he'd had a moment of panic that had nothing to do with anyone. Sometimes, it was hard work being a mess. He always tried keeping everything in his little sphere perfect and overwhelmed himself for no reason. He took another breath.

Legend and Leo exchanged another glance and a laughing smile. He felt like he had missed something, but the air lightened. "I have to get going, guys. Call me if either of you need anything. I need to head out before I pass out."

Adrik nodded at Legend's claim. It made sense he would be tired after staying up all night. Once he was gone, Adrik focused on Leo.

Leo seemed to be in his own head. He shook his head. His gaze met Adrik's. Everything righted itself. Leo shuffled closer. Adrik's back collided with the counter. Leo's body molded against Adrik's. Adrik's chin lifted. He couldn't look away from Leo's intensity. "You're looking very delicious this morning." Without warning, Leo dipped his head and licked Adrik's neck. "You're making it very hard to concentrate on making breakfast."

Adrik forgot about anything else that wasn't Leo. "I can feel that I'm making things hard."

A soft chuckle rumbled from Leo. His smile held Adrik captivated. He was the reason for Leo's happiness. Adrik's heart squeezed. Not everything he did was a mess. Somehow, he had made this man love him. That was beautiful. His relationship with Leo was like a bright flower growing in the center of a dead field. The grass of Adrik's life had been intentionally poisoned years ago, and it didn't make sense for this one thing to thrive, but—somehow —it did.

"Do you think anyone would notice if we disappeared?" Adrik surprised even himself with the question, but once it was out there, he couldn't stop. "What if we just went back to bed and stayed there?" He could easily disappear inside this bubble with Leo.

Leo kissed the corner of Adrik's mouth. His

breath brushed over Adrik's cheek. Everything felt perfect in that moment.

"I would die the happiest of men," Leo answered. "But that wouldn't be fair to everyone else who loves you. So I suppose I have to share occasionally."

Adrik's heart swelled. It was funny. As much as Adrik craved the dream of disappearing with Leo, he loved that Leo wouldn't indulge him. He was free with Leo. Freer than he had ever been in his life, because Leo loved him enough to make him live a normal life. His love was blinding. Adrik was safe.

WITH THE FLASH DRIVE CLUTCHED TO HIS CHEST, Adrik knocked on Justice's office door. He couldn't explain his nervousness. Something felt off. Possibly, it was Leo's insistence on doing this with him—like Adrik was about to learn something that would set him back in his therapy by three years.

"Come."

At Justice's curt order, Adrik let himself inside Justice's office. He felt like every step he took looked as reluctant as it felt. "Hey, Justice." Justice softened the way he always did when he looked at Adrik. "Leo said you wanted me to look at Dmitry's list, and I did, but I don't think I saw whatever it was that you wanted me to see."

Justice nodded and motioned Adrik closer. "Bring it over here and we'll look together."

Adrik looked Leo's way. His nerves were stretched to the point of breaking. Leo winked—like all was fine. Reassured, Adrik passed the list to Justice. He pulled a chair close to Justice and sat, staring over his shoulder and waiting. Digital words filled the screen once Justice plugged in the flash drive. Names, dates, and addresses rolled out. "Did you see anything out of the ordinary?"

As much as Adrik hated to admit it, because he felt dumb, and worried he wasn't answering how Justice expected, Adrik nodded. "I'm not on the list."

Justice leaned away, making room for Adrik to see the screen better. "Yes, you are. See? There's your address." Justice pointed to the name on the list that shared Adrik's address.

Adrik read the name several times. The address, birth date, and first name matched, but the last name was wrong. "That says Adrik Alexandrov. William said my last name is Zhirov." Adrik tried not choke on William's name. "He said my parents were dead and there were no more

Zhirovs left in my line, so I had nothing left to go home to."

Justice nodded. "That's partially true. Your grandfather on your mother's side was a Zhirov, and your parents are dead, but that isn't your last name. It's Alexandrov—like your father."

Adrik blinked. This was all news to him. "How do you know all this?"

"When I had a look at the list the first day, I made some quiet inquiries. You are Adrik Alexandrov, born February third, nineteen ninety-nine."

Even though Adrik heard every word Justice said, it wouldn't penetrate. "But your last name is Alexandrov."

Justice never looked away. He looked hopeful but also sad—like he didn't know which way to go. "That's because I was old enough to remember my real last name when I was brought to this country, unlike my brothers. Unlike you."

Adrik's heart slammed against the wall of his chest. His gaze shot toward Leo. Leo looked every bit as floored as Adrik. "I don't understand. Are you saying I'm your brother?"

Justice's expression turned pained—like every word he spoke hurt his throat. "I didn't know about you. You were born long after I'd already been sold. It seems our parents enjoyed a rich life of churning out children for profit before they died. We're not the only two."

"What? There are more of us?" Adrik was having a damn hard time wrapping his brain around any of this.

"Just one more living."

Adrik's throat swelled. His nose burned. He could barely breathe or talk around the knowledge he had siblings. "You're my brother." Adrik covered his mouth as tears filled his eyes. He stared at Justice through a haze, trying to come to grips with this new reality. Emotion burst from him in the only way he knew how. Adrik hugged Justice. In truth, he kind of exploded into a hug that nearly knocked Justice from his seat.

"Sorry," Adrik babbled, backing away and patting Justice down, looking for injuries.

Justice motioned for him to calm down. He wore a bright smile completely at odds with Justice's personality. "I'm happy too, angel. I didn't think I had anyone but Whiskey." He hesitated—as if he didn't know if he should keep going or how to express himself. "I know that we already know each other, but I want to know you better. If you're okay with this, I'd like to be your brother. I mean, I know I am, but I want to actually be your brother."

Adrik couldn't stop the tears. He hated that he was such a crier over everything. Leo circled the desk and rubbed his shoulders, lending him strength. "I'd like that."

To Adrik's surprise, Justice's expression turned pained. "I didn't know about you. If I had, I never would've let anything bad happen to you. I hope you know that."

Adrik rushed to reassure him. He couldn't let Justice believe he had any responsibility for Adrik's past. "Don't even think that," Adrik said, rubbing Justice's arm. "I don't want you to start down that road, okay?"

As Justice nodded, his gaze slid toward the door. Adrik looked over his shoulder, spotting Yaro. Yaro pulled a face. "Sorry for the interruption. Zander needs to speak with Leo."

Adrik glanced up. Leo squeezed his shoulders. "Will you be okay for a few minutes?"

"Of course." Adrik patted his hand, trying to reassure him. "Go." He flashed Justice a watery smile. "I'm going to spend some time with my brother." Even he heard the pride in his voice. Leo kissed the top of his head and moved for the door.

Adrik watched him go because he couldn't stop himself. His gaze always followed the piece of his heart that lived outside his body. Today, he felt full. There had not been many times in his life that Adrik had blessings on his side. He felt the luck raining down on him today. Adrik prayed this didn't mean something horrible was about to happen to him. He wasn't the best at not looking a gift horse in the mouth.

AS MUCH AS LEO HATED LEAVING ADRIK WHEN he had just had the news of a lifetime dropped on him, Leo knew Yaro wouldn't let him say no. At least Yaro was looking at him again. That was a step in the right direction.

Zander glanced up from his computer as Leo cleared the door. "Hey. Please close that behind you."

Judging by Zander's cool tone, Leo hoped he would get to leave this room. He pulled the door closed. Yaro joined Pytor on the couch in the corner. Leo chose the seat across from Zander. His huge desk sat between them. Zander didn't look upset. In fact, he seemed more relaxed than Leo had seen him in a long time.

Thankfully, Zander didn't make him fish to find out what was going on. "I think these last few days have proven—when it comes to Adrik—it really does take a village," Zander said, focusing on Leo and pinning him in place with his stare. "You can't deny, with everyone around and someone always focused on him, Adrik has done great the past twenty-four hours."

Leo had a bad feeling growing in his gut. He didn't know how he would handle it if Zander was about to try to insert himself between Adrik and him. "Yes." Even Leo heard the reluctance in his response.

Zander gave him a sharp nod. "I'd like for the two of you to move into my place on a permanent basis." He didn't pose the words as a question. They sounded like an order.

Leo opened his mouth, ready to shut this down, but his confusion spilled out instead. "What?"

Zander leaned back in his chair. A kind smile hovered on his lips. "Yaro has a huge soft spot for Adrik."

"This is true," Yaro said, chiming in from the corner.

Zander ignored the interruption. "And as much as we've enjoyed your connection to the police department these past few years, it's only a matter of time before your connections to us becomes too deep to go unnoticed."

"I don't know about that." Leo was pretty good at keeping his head down.

"Do you plan to marry Adrik?" Zander asked without missing a beat.

"Yes." Leo didn't hesitate because Adrik deserved to have all of Leo. A full and real life.

Zander kept pushing. "He's Justice's brother. Justice's husband has already lost his job by association. Do you really want to cast doubt on your old cases?"

No. He couldn't have that. Leo would land in prison. "What are you suggesting?"

"Come work for me full time. Stay with us and dedicate your whole focus on helping Adrik finish school and regain his confidence. When he's ready, I'll have two new full-time employees. I assure you no one will even notice two new additions to my home."

Leo shook his head, trying to absorb Zander's demands. He didn't mistake this moment for a second as being a request. Leo wasn't sure what would happen if he said no. "This is a lot, Zander. On the surface, everything you say makes sense. There's nothing I'd rather do than dedicate myself full time to Adrik, but I have to be honest. This sounds a lot like a soul trade. Nothing is ever free and someday the bill will come due on this. What do you really expect in return?"

For a full minute, Zander stared at him in silence before sitting forward. His gaze never wavered. "Nothing." He made it hard to doubt his sincerity. There was honesty in his eyes. "I started down this path, hoping to make right all of Gio's wrongs that I could. I haven't fixed Adrik until you fix Adrik. He needs Justice, and Yaro, and you. This job gives him purpose and I need you both. Do this for him. You'll never want for a thing in my employ."

Leo didn't want for a thing in the man's part-time employ. He couldn't imagine what working for him full time would be like. Leo couldn't agree without talking to Adrik. Adrik might not want to give up the familiarity and safety of his home. "How about this? I'll ask Adrik. If he agrees, then I'm in."

"That's all I can ask."

Leo had to hand it to Zander. He didn't gloat. Leo didn't know many men who would have passed up that chance. Of course, Zander was so accustomed to having his way, he might not have thought there was any chance Leo would say no. As much as Leo didn't want to quit his job and move, he saw Zander's point. Adrik wasn't progressing as quickly with only part of Leo's focus. Between his position on the force and the part time-work he did for Zander, Adrik had—somewhat—fallen to the wayside, barely participating in his online classes and counseling. Leo needed to fix that. He would talk to Adrik. Who knew? Maybe he was about to have his angel full time. That sounded almost too good to be true. First, he had a plan to set into motion. With a promise to think about Zander's offer, Leo made his way back to Justice's office. He found Adrik and Justice huddled behind Justice's computer. They looked up as Leo crossed the threshold. Adrik flashed him an adorable smile. His eyes were still red, but he looked happy. The sight warmed Leo's heart.

"Hey," Justice said, greeting him. "We have a thought to run by you. Adrik says you're considering taking some vacation time. How do you feel about the two of you joining Whiskey and me for a week in Vegas? I'd love to spend some time with Adrik, and we could go speak with our other brother."

Leo's brow furrowed. He felt it happen. "Your other living sibling is in Vegas?"

The pair exchanged a glance. Adrik was the one who answered. "It's Dmitry."

Trying to act surprised wasn't easy. He had known those eerily light-colored eyes of Dmitry's had looked familiar. Between Adrik and Justice, he had looked at those same eyes every day for years. "Wow. Well. I don't know what to say." He was in love with a man who had two professional killers as brothers. It was a damn good thing he was too in love with Adrik to feel the least bit intimidated. "Yeah. If Adrik wants to go, we're in." Adrik's smile made everything worthwhile. Now he just needed to make it to Vegas without Adrik finding out this trip had been his idea.

SEVEN

VEGAS WAS HOT AND LOUD. If not for Leo, Adrik wouldn't have had the courage to come here. It wasn't as bad this time around. Adrik thought he might be getting better. Even though he was thrilled to learn he had two brothers, and he was equally certain Dmitry had known that when he had given Adrik that list, he wasn't sure how they would be received. Justice had gone to see Dmitry without Adrik. They had decided together that would be best. Justice could hold his own if the news wasn't received well. Adrik openly acknowledged he could not. He tried not to pace the floor while he waited to see how things went. Leo kept casting Adrik reassuring glances. Adrik recognized how lucky he was to have Leo.

"I love you." Adrik didn't feel like he had anything else to offer.

Leo smiled like that was all he needed. "I—" His phone rang, cutting Leo off. "It's Justice." Adrik held his breath as Leo answered. "Hello?" Adrik didn't look away from Leo. He didn't as much as blink. "Yeah. Okay. We're on our way." Leo shoved his phone in his pocket. "Come on, baby. Justice and Dmitry are downstairs, waiting in one of the dining halls for us."

A smile he couldn't contain exploded across Adrik's face. "Really? He came?"

Leo shuffled closer. He rubbed Adrik's arms. "It seems so."

Adrik took a deep breath. He was happy, but he didn't know if he should be. It was possible Dmitry had shown to tell them to stay away. Adrik pressed his lips to Leo's, needing his strength. He immediately felt like a new person, especially when he felt Leo smile against his lips. It was like he breathed in Leo's happiness.

"I didn't get to tell you I love you too," Leo whispered against his lips.

That was it. He was recharged to a hundred percent because Leo loved him. "I'm ready."

Leo linked fingers with him. "Then your escort awaits."

Adrik swallowed a chuckle as they headed for the elevator. They stopped on the third floor. Adrik shot him a questioning look.

Leo shrugged. "They decided to book a private dining area. Dmitry doesn't go in public often."

"Oh. Okay." That made sense. Dmitry had wiped out the entire mafia family in charge of Vegas. He wouldn't want to visit a Luna public restaurant. When they reached the private dining hall, Adrik's jaw dropped. The place looked like it had been decorated for a high school prom, except a little classier. Not that Adrik had ever been to prom. The gorgeous flowers and champagne aside, everyone he considered family was there, including people who really were related to him. Dmitry had brought his husband, Jozsua, and their son. Zander was there with Maverick, Pytor, and Yaro. Even Legend had shown. He had thought only Justice and Whiskey would be joining them for lunch with Dmitry. He had no idea what was happening. There was a guy he didn't know standing away from the group. He looked like a businessman of some type. Everyone looked their way, openly expectant.

Adrik's gaze slid Leo's way.

Leo was smiling. He rubbed the back of his neck, looking guilty as hell. "How do you feel about a surprise wedding?"

Adrik blinked. "For who?"

Leo's eyes danced with laughter. "Well, I kind of hoped for you and me."

The spurt of pure joy that hit Adrik was indescribable. He never, ever dreamed he would be good enough to be Leo's husband, or anyone's for that matter. Adrik's eyes filled with tears. A lump formed in his throat.

Leo shifted, looking worried. "If you don't want this, I won't be mad. I know I was extremely hopeful. It's just that I wasn't sure I would ever get your brothers together like this again, and I knew you would want them here for this, so I pre-registered us for a marriage license, and Zander arranged for this guy who can handle our paperwork that usually keeps celebrities from having to visit the marriage bureau, but we don't have to do this if this isn't what you want. We can just enjoy a nice party together." Leo rambled like he was certain Adrik would say no. "I just don't ever want you to doubt again that I want to spend the rest of my life with you."

Adrik leapt, nearly unmanning Leo in his enthusiasm. "Yes! I want my surprise wedding." He kissed Leo's face every place he could reach. Adrik could hear the laughter from their friends, but he couldn't stop. He had never been happier in his life. Leo was the most amazing man on the planet.

With his heart racing and life moving at the speed of light, he was rushed through paperwork, and "I do"s he never expected were exchanged in front of the family he thought he would never have. Everything moved so fast, Adrik felt lightheaded and like he hadn't gotten to talk to anyone as long as he wanted. But he also gripped Leo's hand so tightly, he felt sure Leo's fingers would fall off from lack of circulation, and Dmitry promised they would see each other again. Halfway through the night, it dawned on him that he had a nephew now thanks to Dmitry, and in-laws. In a single night, his family had grown by leaps and bounds. Leo's parents lived too far away for Adrik to have met them more than on special occasions. Plus, they didn't really travel, but he had a mother- and father-in-law now. His mind was blown. It was almost too much.

He leaned harder into Leo's side, feeling the weight of the night. Leo's gaze shot his way. Concern swam in his eyes as his gaze moved over Adrik's face. "Time for bed."

Adrik thought to argue. He wanted to fully enjoy

his night. Leo's expression said any denials would be quickly silenced. Not to mention, he kind of liked the idea of going to bed with his husband.

A smile spread across his face.

Leo's expression shifted. Hunger filled his gaze. "Say goodnight."

That was all the warning Adrik got before he found himself hanging from Leo's shoulder. Laughter and applause followed them from the room, keeping Adrik's hot face buried against Leo's back. He was horrified and ecstatic. Leo stroked his ass and Adrik added turned on to the list. Leo was like home base, though. Adrik was safe to do and feel anything with him. Now Leo was his husband. It was surreal as hell.

If anyone witnessed Leo's race to the room with Adrik over his shoulder, Adrik wouldn't know. He never uncovered his face to see, and Leo was too shameless to be bothered by anyone else.

"You can stop hiding now," Leo said, setting Adrik on his feet. They were alone again inside their room. Leo's gaze moved over Adrik's face. "Mr. Humphrey," he added in barely a whisper.

Reality slammed into Adrik at the name. He was someone new. No longer was Adrik the child who had been sold to a monster nor was he the teenager who had been rescued a mess. Adrik was now the man who had married the love of his life. Today, he had a new start. He would make it the best beginning ever.

"This is the life I would've chosen for myself no matter what," Adrik said, as if Leo could hear his thoughts.

Leo nodded, looking serious and intense. "Same. I would've chosen you even if we met passing on the street."

Adrik's eyes burned. Leo always knew what to say. "Thank you for the perfect wedding." It was perfect. If Leo had done things any other way, Adrik recognized he might have buckled under the stress of planning or lost his courage if given too much time of questioning his worth. Leo had taken all that away. He had gifted Adrik with the freedom to live for the moment without the self-sabotage Adrik normally experienced. "How did I get so lucky?"

Leo shuffled closer. His hands slid across Adrik's hips. "I'm the lucky one." He looked hungry. Adrik wanted a full life.

He licked his lips as he stared at Leo's mouth. Leo dipped his head. Adrik rushed to speak up before he lost his chance. "Would you make love to me?"

At Adrik's question, a sexy chuckle rumbled from Leo. "That was my plan."

Adrik leaned away an inch before Leo could kiss him. "I mean, for real. Not just touching." Adrik's cheeks heated, but he didn't take back the request. This was his wedding night. He would only get one of those and he wanted it to be his version of perfect. Adrik needed Leo to do everything he would have done if he had married any other man.

"Are you sure?" Leo was so close, his every breath brushed Adrik's lips.

"Positive."

Adrik's pants loosened beneath Leo's touch. "You can change your mind at any point. I already have everything because I have you."

"I trust you," Adrik said as he swiped his lips across Leo's. His fingers fumbled for the button on Leo's pants. They kissed while slowly undressing each other. There was nothing frantic about their motions. They had the rest of their lives together. Even once they were nude, they didn't immediately move for the bed.

Leo's fingers skimmed up and down Adrik's back as he kissed Adrik's neck. "Tell me what you picture in your mind. There're countless ways to make love. Tell me your version so I can make it real."

Adrik closed his eyes and focused on Leo's touch and the sound of his voice. He didn't want to lose his courage. Leo made him brave. Adrik took a breath, digging deep. "You know what you taught me to do with my fingers? I want to do that to you with my cock."

Leo moaned against his throat. Adrik's dick throbbed at the sound. "You're always welcome to do whatever you want to my body, baby." Leo took his hand and headed for the bed. He stopped and dug through his suitcase, coming out with a small tube before climbing onto the bed. Adrik couldn't look away from Leo's gorgeous body. All the times he had stared at Leo and dreamed rushed to the forefront of Adrik's mind. Leo was about to let him do the things he fantasized about.

As Leo crawled across the mattress and Adrik watched his perfect ass flex with every move, his tongue forgot to be scared. "Maybe later, you could do the same thing to me." Pre-cum rolled down his length at the idea.

Leo settled onto his back. "Come here, sexy. We have all the time in the world to do whatever you want."

Adrik scrambled to join Adrik. He paused several times to kiss parts of Leo's body as he crawled between Leo's thighs. His teeth found Leo's nipple. He couldn't stop himself from lightly nibbling. The way Leo's back arched, chasing Adrik's mouth, was hot as hell. Adrik fought the urge to stroke himself.

As if Leo understood, he pressed the tube of lube into Adrik's hand. "Take this, sexy. Coat your cock. The slicker we are, the easier this will be.

Adrik didn't pass up the opportunity to stroke himself, coating his dick. Since his hand was still covered in lube, he played with Leo's ass, getting him slick too. Leo spread his legs, writhing beneath his touch like Adrik had him aroused beyond insanity. In fact, Leo's cock dripped pre-cum all over his stomach and Adrik couldn't look away from the sight. He had done that. He was the reason Leo burned. It was the most empowering moment of Adrik's life.

Using his fingers, Adrik got a bit carried away. He found that spot Leo told him about and massaged. The wilder Leo got beneath his touch, the bolder Adrik felt. He moved higher. With Leo's knees spread wide, Adrik got as close as he could and swiped his crown across Leo's asshole. It felt good—like tiny spasms danced through his erection. He wanted to know what it felt like to be inside Leo. Adrik wanted to find the man's soul with his dick and touch it. He eased inside, wanting to savor the moment. Adrik was so focused on watching his hands and savoring every sensation that he didn't feel any embarrassment. It was like he had disappeared inside his own tiny world where he was free to do whatever he pleased. Every moan, cry, and whimper from Leo drove him deeper. Adrik stayed focused on finding that internal bump with his cock. He wanted to rub his dick against it.

The sound Leo made when Adrik found it nearly stole an orgasm from Adrik. He had to close his eyes and breathe to stop from coming right then. Adrik wasn't ready for this to be over. He was enjoying himself too much. It was like he had stepped inside a fantasy and he was different here. Strong. His cock jumped, reminding him of how crazed he was to have Leo like this. Adrik's hips rolled. He thrust, needing to hear Leo make that sound again. Leo cried Adrik's name and something inside Adrik broke. He found his rhythm, massaging Leo's insides with his dick. Adrik's focus was completely locked on every sensation happening to his erection. He held Leo's thighs and stared at Leo's dick. Adrik thrust over and over, watching. Waiting. Anticipating the moment Leo blew. He didn't want to miss the sight of cum pumping from Leo's beautiful cock.

The way Leo strained made Adrik wonder if he should rub Leo's erection to help relieve him. Before Adrik could decide, Leo stiffened and cum shot from his dick. His asshole sucked Adrik deeper unexpectedly. Adrik gasped as the move massaged an orgasm from him. He thrust harder, chasing the pleasure. He had never felt anything like it. Adrik was half insane with the need to hang on to the sensation. He thought he might be addicted already to the way it felt to be inside Leo—connected. They were one on a level he had never shared with anyone else. He never wanted to experience this with anyone else. This was special. In fact, the idea of Leo ever feeling this way with anyone else nearly snapped his mind. He understood then why Leo had been so angry about Legend kissing him. If anyone else ever put their lips on Leo, Adrik would cut their damn lips from their body. He had never felt more possessive in his life.

"Goddamn. You look fierce as hell."

At Leo's claim, Adrik's gaze shot to his. Those amber eyes he loved so much watched his every move, reminding him he wasn't invisible. For the first time in his life, Adrik wasn't the least bit shy or embarrassed. He just wanted more. He crawled up Leo's body without breaking eye contact. He couldn't smile or look away. He felt every bit as fierce as Leo claimed he appeared.

"I love you," Adrik growled. He needed Leo to understand how powerful he felt about them. Without giving Leo time to return the words, he kissed Leo, pouring his heart into it. He swore his love poured from him and into Leo as their tongues brushed. His entire body moved against Leo, matching the rhythm of his tongue. Leo massaged him every place he could reach—as if he felt the same crazed desire to mold perfectly against each other but incapable of being still with the overwhelming emotions racing.

"Jesus, I love you," Leo whispered between kisses and Adrik's heart was full. He finally found exactly what he needed to settle into Leo's hold. When Leo's arms tightened around him, Adrik realized his entire body shook. He was overcome.

For what felt like hours, they didn't move. Leo held him and Adrik soaked in his affection. He felt like a sponge, absorbing everything he had been denied before Leo.

Finally, Leo kissed his forehead. "I know it's been a full day for you, filled with changes, but I need to talk to you about one more."

Adrik's chin lifted. He needed to see Leo's face

at the uncertainty in his voice. "You can talk to me about anything. It's my job."

The smile that touched Leo's lips at Adrik's claim warmed Adrik's heart. He looked proud and happy. "Zander made me an offer, but I told him I won't do anything until I talk to you. I want us to decide together."

"Okay." Leo's tone worried him a little.

"I need to leave my job before I get busted tampering with evidence for Zander." Adrik's throat tightened. He had never considered the possibility, but it was a real threat to them. Adrik couldn't lose Leo. Thankfully, Leo kept talking and easing Adrik's fear. "Zander offered me full-time work with him. Actually, he offered us both full-time jobs, on the condition that we move in with him, and that I help you graduate while Yaro works with you on learning to defend yourself."

This was a lot of modifications at once, but they were good changes. Adrik would have Leo full time. They would be completely safe living with Zander. Zander was practically untouchable, and his house was like a fortress. They had been invited to become part of Zander's family. He never had to be afraid again. "Wow."

"I know. It's a lot," Leo said, sounding worried.

"If you don't want to move from the home we have now, just say the word and I'll tell Zander no."

"No." Adrik didn't want Leo getting the wrong impression. Excitement raced through him. "We get to be together all the time and I'll never have to look over my shoulder. Wow," he repeated, incapable of voicing his thoughts. His gaze shot to Leo's as another side of things hit. "But how do you feel about this? I mean, it's your house we'd be leaving. You'd be giving up everything."

Leo shook his head. "You are everything to me. I'd be gaining more of you. That sounds like heaven to me."

Adrik went on the attack, leaping onto Leo's body. He tried hugging and kissing every place he could reach. Laughter shook Leo's body at his antics, only making Adrik more outrageous. His life was so damn full that Adrik couldn't think straight. He couldn't see past the happiness. Leo had done that for him—filled him to the point of taking away the nightmares. He would never stop trying to do the same for Leo. As long as they lived, Adrik would make Leo happy. Their future looked filled with light.

. . .

Keep an eye out for the next book in the Sugar Daddies series, *Sugar Guards*.

If you'd like to read Dmitry and Jozsua's book, it's part of my No Rival series, *Uncaged*.

Please consider leaving a review at the retailer where this book was purchased. Reviews really help with a book's visibility, which ensures I can continue writing. Thank you, Charity.

ABOUT THE AUTHOR

Charity Parkerson is an award winning and multi-published author with several companies. Born with no filter from her brain to her mouth, she decided to take this odd quirk and insert it in her characters.

*Eight-time Readers' Favorite Award Winner
    *2015 Passionate Plume Award Finalist
    *2013 Reviewers' Choice Award Winner
    *2012 ARRA Finalist for Favorite Paranormal Romance
    *Five-time winner of The Mistress of the Darkpath

Connect with her online:

--Join   my   street   team:
facebook.com/TeamCharityParkerson
    --Website: charityparkerson.com
    --Facebook:
facebook.com/authorCharityParkerson

facebook.com/TheMenofSin

--Twitter: twitter.com/CharityParkerso